A division of Hodder Headline Limited

All characters in this publication are fictitious and any resemblance to real persons, living or dead, is purely coincidental.

A Catalogue record for this book is available from the British Library

ISBN 0 340 89447 4

Typeset in Goudy by Avon DataSet Ltd, Bidford-on-Avon, Warwickshire

Printed and bound in Great Britain by Bookmarque Ltd, Croydon, Surrey

The paper and board used in this paperback by Hodder Children's Books are natural recyclable products made from wood grown in sustainable forests. The manufacturing processes conform to the environmental regulations of the country of origin.

Hodder Children's Books
a division of Hodder Headline Ltd
338 Euston Road
London NW1 3BH

Acknowledgements

I would like to acknowledge *Culpeper's Complete Herbal* by Nicholas Culpeper, 1616–1654 and also *Restoration London, Everyday Life in London 1660–1670* by Lisa Picard. I would not have been able to write this story without reference to these books.

I would also like to thank my writing friends Christine Purkis and Amanda Mitchison for all their encouragement and enthusiasm. Also, thanks to my non-writing husband Keith Erskine, for absolutely everything.

For T. J. E.

1

1682

Kidnapped

Reuben had been walking for so long now that every tree or stone he passed on the lonely lane swayed in front of his eyes. And the terrible image in his mind – the body dangling on a rope – *that* was swaying too, back and forth, back and forth, like a giant, ragged pendulum.

Reuben shook his head, trying to dislodge the pictures, but the muddy lane was pitted with holes and peppered with stones and he stumbled. He stopped to rub at his sore ankles where his boots had chafed him. His arms felt leaden, as if he'd been carrying invisible pails of milk for the last three miles. He wrapped them around his chest, digging his cold hands into the warm nest of his armpits before he trudged off again, not knowing where he was going or what would make him stop.

His thoughts seesawed in time to the bobbing horizon of hedge, tree and ditch:

Granny's gone. I hate them. She's gone. I hate them. She's gone. His fists clenched and unclenched: hate them, hate them, hate them!

He walked and walked.

Since he'd left the village, he'd hardly met a soul. Every time he did see another figure on the road his heart started beating wildly and sweat wetted his hands: was it the churchwarden's men coming to catch him? Or Meg Silver? Her big son, Oliver? The magistrate? Every person posed a threat.

I'll say I'm John Tavener from Portsmouth, going to meet an uncle. John Tavener from Portsmouth. Don't forget, he chided himself. John Tavener.

He pulled his hat down low; it was in a sorry state after the rain and sleeping outside. The wide brim dipped and flared wildly and the green ribbon that his grandmother had sewn round it had completely vanished, but it could still hide his face from passersby.

Swing, swing, back and forth, went the pendulum. *Swish, swish*, her skirts sighed and sang as they swayed from side to side, and the thick rope creaked against the wood.

Three times, Reuben was convinced there were soft footsteps shadowing his. Each time he glanced round, squinting into the low sunshine, but if there was anyone, they always dipped out of sight just as he turned. So he gave up looking round and didn't even hear the horse clip-clopping along behind him, or the grinding sound of the cart's wooden wheels rumbling along, until they were too close for him to run.

He'd thought he was alert to any danger and yet he'd let a cart creep up on him.

Stupid boy! Dolt!

He went on, staring down at his muddy boots, seeing the path slide past his feet like a belt slipping through its loops.

Now the cart was right behind him. His heart began to pound. A giant hand squeezed iron fingers around his chest.

'Way! Halt there!'

Reuben faltered, his feet seemed to jolt against the earth. He stopped and the leafless trees beside him suddenly stilled long enough for him to see them clearly and automatically start naming them; birch; alder – damp in that spot, though it didn't look it; elm; hazel . . . Anything rather than face another human being.

The horse snorted loudly, shook its head, jangling the metal on its harness. Reuben felt a wave of warmth against his back, steaming off the animal's flanks and was surprised when tears pricked his eyes.

'Where you going, boy? Want to take the weight off them spindly legs?'

Not men from the village to bring him back, then. Reuben turned and looked up at the big, piebald horse and tall, covered wagon. A man and a youth were perched on it like scraggy birds.

The youth's lumpen and misshapen head put Reuben

in mind of an unbaked loaf of bread; his small, dark eyes pushed into the doughy flesh, like shrivelled currants. His cheeks were raw with spots and sores; his hair a mess of oily rat-tails. He grinned a crooked-toothed grin at Reuben and nodded in greeting.

The other, older man was very different. Although he was grinning at Reuben too, his smile didn't lighten his strange face. The man's massive nose, like a broken, hooked beak, curved lopsidedly. The left cheek was dented and scarred; the left eye hung slightly more open than his right, as if a weight were hanging on the lower lid. His coal-black eyes must have been staring straight into Reuben's and yet they went past him, through him and out the other side like a red-hot needle burning a hole through a leather strap. The eyes were stony, dark as jet, set deep under jutting brows. Beneath a tall, battered old hat, curling, wiry hair streaked with grey fell to his shoulders.

Reuben swayed, trying to ignore the throbbing pain in his feet.

'Weary? Come on, lad. We'll give you a ride.' The man with the lopsided face didn't look at Reuben as he spoke, but gazed off down the road as if he could see something very interesting at the end of it. 'It's a long, long walk to Longford,' he added with a chuckle.

'Well–' Before Reuben's protest was past his lips, they were reaching down to him and hauling him up onto the wooden bench, squashing him between them, into a space barely wide enough for a cat.

'Name's Doctor Flyte,' said the man with the terrible face, looking straight ahead. 'Travelling Medical Man. And that lumpen ignoramus is Baggs. Get on, Nellie!' He flicked the reins and Nellie obediently walked on. 'Something bad happen to you, boy?'

Reuben pulled his hat even lower. 'Nothing,' he said. 'I was just walking.'

Baggs nudged him with his elbow. 'You look sad, though. Or is it that your ma was so ugly, you took your first look at her when you were borned and got that snitchy face, eh?'

'I'm sure she wasn't ugly,' said Reuben, miserably.

'Least ways he's known his ma,' said Doctor Flyte, 'which is more than you can claim, Baggs.'

Baggs snorted.

'Peculiar,' said Doctor Flyte, staring at Nellie's back, 'seeing you on the road. We've not so long heard of a boy whose grandma's been hanged for witchcraft. That boy was walking from Willsbridge . . . Coincidence, ain't it?'

'Don't know.' Reuben swallowed, too tired and depressed to invent a lie. He shook his head. He felt Flyte and Baggs exchange a look over his head and knew they didn't believe him; he closed his eyes.

And I don't care, he said silently. I don't care what you two think. I don't care about anything in the world.

The wagon swayed and rocked from side to side as it trundled along the uneven track, pitching Reuben against his companions. Something tumbled out of its place in the back of the covered cart, making Reuben glance round instinctively, but Flyte quickly snatched the thick leather curtains closed behind him.

'Never you mind,' he growled. 'Not your business, lad.'

Reuben didn't care. Keep your secrets, he thought, and I'll keep mine.

The wagon had a rounded roof of patched leather stretched over hoops of wood. Its curved sides were covered by thick cloths, under which Reuben glimpsed colourful writing. Inside the wagon itself, there were shelves lined with bottles, packets of powders and swinging bunches of herbs. Flyte was a medical man, he'd said, and that stuff reminded Reuben of an apothecary's shop. Apothecary. Huh! He'd surely made a bad choice in travelling companions.

Reuben crouched lower, as if he could make himself invisible. His bony bottom jarred painfully on the hard seat as the wagon tossed him about.

I should've just gone on and on, he thought. Wish I'd not taken the ride. Wish the horse had run right over me. Wish I'd gone on walking till my feet had worn out. Wish I'd just fallen dead in a ditch.

2
Reuben is Given a Gift

'Longford,' growled Doctor Flyte as the wagon rolled into the town. 'You won't have seen the like, I 'spect.'

'Never,' Reuben heard himself whisper.

He sat up on his hard seat and stared about, sniffing the air like a hound, peering at everything around him. For the first time since it had happened, he forgot about his grandmother.

Reuben imagined the wagon was like a boat, clearing folk out of the way like a boat cleaves the water. The dogs dodged its rumbling wheels and children scurried past, criss-crossing in front of the horses with sure-footed swiftness. Crows and ravens, strutting over the dung heaps and scraps in the road, rose squawking as they passed, then floated back behind them.

Reuben's village, Birtwell Priory, was a jumble of small cottages strung along muddy tracks and paths, with three farms and a church. This place was so much bigger! The houses were so fine, some joined together forming a sort of crenellated castle wall with glass gleaming in the windows and painted doors. Some houses leaned drunkenly into the street. There were narrow, cobbled lanes leading into dark, higgledy-piggledy alleyways cluttered with hanging signs and, everywhere, horses, carts, coaches and noise.

The wagon sailed on through the sea of living things. Rich men in leather boots with silver buckles and glorious hats plumed with long feathers. Wealthy women wearing blue and red cloth with lace and gold thread. Ordinary folk like himself, in brown and black. All shouting, jostling, talking, laughing. Pigs tethered on ropes. Cows, children, chickens, pigeons. Hundreds of tradesmens' signs, squeaking as they blew back and forth in the breeze: a cradle showed a basket maker's, a bag of nails for the ironmonger's, Adam and Eve, sharing an apple, advertised the fruit seller.

The noise was incredible! Reuben covered his ears with his hands. In his tiny village there was nothing louder than the church bells – though Mister Smith was famous for his rowdiness after drinking too much mead and the cattle made a terrible noise when their calves were taken, still it was quiet compared with this.

The smell! Reuben pinched his nose with his fingers. A long, narrow gutter ran down the centre of the road, piled with rotting food scraps, bones, stable manure and human waste. When Flyte and Baggs saw him trying to block out the offending smells, they laughed and elbowed him roughly. He'd almost forgotten them – now their nearness and strangeness sent his heart hammering.

I was a fool to have come! A fool to have taken their offer of a ride! Look at this place! Oh, what's to become of me? Where'll I go, Granny? Where?

How poor some of the children were! There were ragged, homeless boys and girls like him, like shadows, hanging back, clutching the walls, lurking in darkened doorways and corners, watching through half opened, shifting eyes. His heart lifted suddenly: why I could disappear here easily, like a rat down a hole – if I was brave enough to try.

'We'll be stopping the night. I've some business here,' Doctor Flyte said without looking at him. 'You stay with Baggs. Buy the boy a thick cloak, Baggs. Spare no expense. He's cold and the nights are colder.'

'I haven't money to pay you back,' said Reuben quickly.

'That's not a worry.'

'Are there places here that sell cloaks then?' he asked, peering around.

'Yes,' said Baggs. 'Plenty of shops.'

There weren't any shops in Birtwell Priory.

Why would they buy me a cloak? Reuben wondered. He tried not to care, not to thrill at the idea, but a cloak! A new cloak! Despite everything, it was exciting.

They drove first to an inn. It was a low-roofed building with black timbers making a pattern of diagonals and uprights against white-painted walls. The wagon went through an archway and into a courtyard at the back where several men and boys were busy with horses, carts, bags of provisions and barrels of beer. A red-faced maid with no front teeth leaned out of an upper window and waved her cloth at them.

Flyte waved back and blew her a kiss with a wet, smacking sound.

Reuben had never seen a building so grand. He looked up at the letters above the door.

'The Longford Arms,' he read slowly.

Doctor Flyte grabbed his arm. 'You can read letters, boy?'

'Oh, just a bit, sir,' said Reuben, nervous that he might sound superior. 'My grandmother – I never went to school, but she taught me so I could study. The Bible,' he added, though in truth it was to read her recipes and potions.

'You can read. Write too, eh?' Doctor Flyte eyed him with suspicion. Reuben nodded. 'Well, mind you don't let anyone else know,' Flyte snapped. 'You're not the sort that should be a-reading and a-writing.'

At the side of the inn was a large barn with stabling for horses. They left Nellie and the wagon there.

Flyte signalled to the stable boy to approach. 'Boy! Here! Name?'

'William, sir.'

'William. That's a fine name. You're to watch my horse, William, and my caravan here. Nobody must touch my belongings,' he told him. 'Do as I say, and I'll give you two pennies now and another two tomorrow.'

'No, sir. Yes, sir.'

'Very valuable herbs, books and the like.' Doctor Flyte tapped the side of his nose. 'Needs watching.' He turned to Baggs. 'I've an appointment with Mister Wilkes for bottles,' he said. 'Mister Smith for a new shirt and Mister Gifford, the apothecary, for some interesting powders . . .'

Apothecary. Apothecary.

In a sudden rush, Reuben saw the gnome-like old apothecary in Lower Birtwell; a gnarled old man, colourless like a dried up root and just as useless. He clenched his fists. If only I were bigger and stronger and older, he thought, I'd go back and kill him! If only . . .

3
Sarah

When his grandmother had first been accused of being a witch, Reuben had gone to the apothecary, begging him to help.

'Oh, please, sir, Mister Gowdie, please!' he'd cried, falling to his knees and clutching at the man's jacket. 'Just a few words in her favour, couldn't you? You used to like her. You talked potions and mixtures and . . . Didn't she ease your wife's gout? Didn't she? If you could just come to Willsbridge and . . .'

Mister Gowdie had looked round nervously. 'Now, boy, please!' He'd clamped his spider-like hand on Reuben's shoulder and pushed him out of his cottage. 'Go away. Go away. You know I can't help. Hush, hush, and go away.' Reuben had heard the bolts being dragged across the closed door.

He'd knocked and kicked and yelled at the door, but it was no good. Gowdie hadn't opened it again. He had been Reuben's only hope.

'Why won't you help me?' Reuben had yelled at the shut door. 'I need your help!'

Mister Gowdie's bald head had bobbed up at the window, but only to shoo Reuben away. Reuben had waited all afternoon, but Mister Gowdie didn't show himself again.

Apothecaries cannot be trusted. If I ever have to deal with another apothecary in my life, Reuben thought, it will only be to curse him.

Baggs grabbed hold of him. 'You stick with me, Scabby,' he said, gripping Reuben tightly round the top of his arm. 'Come on.' He dragged Reuben back into the streets of the town.

Reuben was tossed and tumbled, battered and squashed. Boys ran, zigzagging along, selling papers, calling and waving to people they knew. One crashed into him, sending him spinning into a small, dirty man covered in swathes of dead rats.

'Rats to kill? Any rats to kill?' cried the man, waving his placard angrily at Reuben. Reuben felt the smooth whiplash of a rat's tail swish against his bare hand before he managed to get away.

The noise of the crowd rose up around them like a great wave.

'Sweet cakes to buy!'

'Fresh rabbits! Fresh rabbits for sale!'

'Who'll buy my lavender?'

'Hey!' Reuben bounced off one vendor only to knock into another.

'Have a care! Mind my glass!' Creamy glass flasks with

bulbous round bases were strung all over his body, as if he was sprouting strange, pendulous mushrooms. 'Glass! Clear glass for sale!'

Bemused, exhausted and incapable of action, Reuben let Baggs pull him along the street.

They passed a baker's shop where the smell of hot meat pies from the ovens was so strong Reuben expected to see it floating out like a colourful ribbon of gravy. He tasted the smells of pastry, hot apples, warm fruits, oranges. His mouth watered, he swallowed hungrily. When had he last eaten?

Baggs paused for a moment in front of a box-maker's shop and Reuben had a second to catch his breath and to pick up a torn fragment of a grubby pamphlet from the street before Baggs yanked him on. The paper was extolling the virtues of coffee:

. . . it closeth the Orifice of the Stomack, and fortifies the heat within. It is very good to help digestion and therefore of great use to be taken about Three or Four o'clock in the Afternoon, as well as in the Morning . . .

There had been a little man who brought pamphlets all the way from London and although they weren't new, they made fine reading, so Reuben's grandmother said. They were about the King and science and new inventions.

Baggs tore the paper from his hand. 'That's devil's talk!' he said, chucking it down. 'Let it be. That's not for us. Don't suppose you've ever seen the likes of this town, eh?' he added.

Reuben shook his head.

'Ever had a new cloak?'

'Yes.' His grandmother had ordered the weaver to make the cloth, then had it cut and sewn. On the inside, by the collar, she had embroidered his initials. It had taken weeks and was to last him years, and Reuben wondered on whose shoulders it was hanging now.

The new cloak that Baggs bought him was of fine dark-green material, the colour of pine needles. Baggs paid for the cloak without a word, then steered Reuben back to the inn, holding him tightly all the way.

When they reached The Longford Arms, Doctor Flyte was already seated in the corner of a large, crowded room beside a roaring fire. A girl was plunging a hot poker into his mug of ale, making it splutter and froth before she set it on the table before him. Flyte's cheeks were flushed and his dark eyes were glistening. His tall, battered hat was tipped over one eye.

'Your cloak to your liking?' he said.

'Thank you, sir, yes. But . . .' Reuben's thoughts were whirling around in a desperate flurry. 'I . . .'

He needed a piss. His bladder was bursting, making him jig up and down, but he dare not ask. The inn was so grand; he'd never been anywhere where you didn't just go in a pot or behind a tree. 'I . . .'

'No, not a word. We're celebrating, ain't we?' said Flyte, winking his good eye at Baggs. He called the innkeeper over. 'Mistress Beaver, we'll take a room, thank you kindly, and the dinner.'

'But . . .' Reuben tried again.

'No, no, don't you fuss, boy.'

Baggs pushed Reuben into the high-backed oak seat beside Flyte, and sat down on the other side of him. 'There! All snug, eh?'

Reuben sighed. Weakness washed over him. He might have been a doll, he felt so useless, with arms and legs of lead, and now the heat from the fire was making him hot and groggy. He was so hungry. Uncomfortable. Sad . . .

He gazed into the fire, watching the yellow and blue flames dancing.

Witches were burned.

Mistress Beaver brought them a vast oval platter of stewed carp and another of roast chicken, its skin golden and crispy. Reuben's eyes grew rounder and rounder. He swallowed nervously as saliva oozed into his mouth and his stomach rumbled. It was more food than he'd seen in days. More food than he'd seen in his life.

The fish was enormous, shining with oils and fragrant with herbs. Reuben's eyes darted from the food to Doctor Flyte, to Baggs and back again as they crunched the bones, chewed the meat, swilling it down with ale; he was amazed at their greed.

'Get on with you, young fellow!' cried Mistress Beaver, handing him a mug of frothy, buttered ale. 'Don't you like my cooking?'

Reuben reluctantly took a small piece of chicken and chewed. It melted in his mouth and he quickly reached for more. Doctor Flyte was watching him.

'Eat, boy, eat before it runs away!'

Mistress Beaver followed the first courses with ox-tongues, cheese, and tansy pudding. Reuben ate. Once he started, he wanted more and more, though the carp was slippery in his mouth and tasted of mud. His stomach pushed painfully against his breeches and up under his ribcage until he was sure he'd burst.

When the meal was finished, Baggs and Flyte, laughing, slapping him on the back as if he were an old friend, half dragged him, half carried him out into the darkness to a place which smelled so bad, Reuben retched. Held up on either side, he pissed at last, without even looking to see his great waterfall as it cascaded into the pit below.

They hauled Reuben up the narrow, wooden inn stairs to a chamber with grubby mattresses laid out on the floor. Three were already occupied with snoring men and a pair of mean-looking dogs who growled at them. Six pigeons were roosting in the beams. Baggs quietly took off Reuben's boots, his woollen stockings, his jerkin and jacket. Reuben closed his eyes and let them.

'What's that?' Flyte said gruffly, grabbing at Reuben, as he collapsed on the mattress. 'Hold him, Baggs.'

Reuben's shirt collar had come undone at the neck, and Flyte pushed it further back, scrabbling at his skin.

'Dirt?' whispered Baggs, rubbing Reuben's grubby skin.

Reuben kept his eyes closed, wanting to shut them out. He knew the mark they meant.

'Birthmark,' said Flyte, quietly. 'Like someone's spilled blood on him.'

'Is that good?' said Baggs as they dropped him onto the mattress and threw a cover over him. 'Nah, it's bad, ain't it?' he added with a touch of hope in his voice.

'It's not important,' growled Flyte.

Reuben lay very still, his eyes half closed, the room spinning off at an angle, swooping and tilting. He'd drunk too much ale; the food had been rich, his insides hurt. Flyte was whispering, he strained to hear, it was something important, he could tell. He squinted up at their towering figures.

'He stays with us, Baggs, and that's an end to it.'

'But, Doctor, I can do everything . . .' Baggs's words slipped away in a meaningless jumble.

'. . . because I want him . . . He's mine . . .' said Flyte shortly.

Reuben didn't like that. He longed for his grandmother and the safety of their little cottage in Birtwell Priory.

Or, since that was not to be, then death.

He felt Flyte and Baggs settling down, sandwiching him between them. The stench of their foul bodies, the filthy mattress, the smoke and ale which seemed to have soaked into the very fabric of the building, was sickening, but he couldn't move.

He was trapped.

4
The Dog in the Barn

'William? William, you damn lazy little fogger! Where are you?' Flyte tore into the barn like a gust of wind, slamming the door against the wall and kicking a bucket over the cobbles.

The stable boy quickly uncurled himself from his straw bed amongst the horses and came forward, blinking. 'Mornin', sirs.'

'Don't mornin' me, knuckle-head. See to my horse!' Flyte gave Reuben a push. 'Reuben! Are you a lazy do-nothing as well? Get the nag ready! Now!'

Reuben scuttled over to help get Nellie fitted into her harness.

'Is that quack your da'?' William leaned down to whisper to Reuben under the horse's chin.

Reuben shook his head.

'Phew! Thank the Lord for small mercies, eh? He's like the Devil, ain't he?' hissed William. 'And behaves like one too! What you to him, then?'

Reuben felt Flyte watching him and shrugged. 'Don't know.'

The horse and wagon were ready. Flyte pushed Reuben up the steps. 'Get up, Reuben. Get on.'

Just before the two of them got up beside him, Reuben caught sight of something slipping through the shadows of the barn: a large, untidy dog, some sort of leggy wolfhound with a shaggy, grey coat. Intrigued, Reuben watched it skulking around behind the horse stalls and bales of hay. It moved stealthily, as if afraid of being seen.

Suddenly, as if it knew it was being watched, the dog stopped. It gazed back at Reuben over its shoulder and its ears softened, its head went down and a light came into its eyes, as if it thought it knew Reuben or remembered him.

Reuben smiled back, until it occurred to him, an instant later, that the dog must have confused him with someone else. The dog loved someone: William maybe; some boy, but not Reuben.

The stab of regret was like a blade slicing his ribs. I'm nothing, he thought. No one. The real Reuben has been left behind. He shook his head at the dog. You don't know me. Nobody does.

Baggs stowed their belongings in the back of the wagon and led the horse out into the yard. As he pushed open the door, light flooded across the hay-strewn floor, but when Reuben looked back into the barn, the dog had gone.

A lump rose in his throat. Wish I were William, living snug here in the barn with that big dog for my friend. He sniffed and bit down on his trembling lip.

Nobody spoke as the wagon lurched and rumbled down the road. Baggs sat idly picking at his spots, his large lower lip hanging loose. Doctor Flyte sat poker-straight and puffed on a long clay pipe, sending streams of evil-smelling smoke straight into Reuben's face.

The sky grew brighter and a weak sun came out. The cold air cut Reuben's cheeks and stung his eyes till they streamed cold tears but his body was warm, squashed as it was between his companions again.

What have I done? he wondered. Why am I here? He looked down at his own small, thin, dirty hands, clutching the edges of his new cloak round him. Skin and bones. No willpower! What would Granny say? Think, boy, think, she'd say, and if you don't want to be with them, get away. You are your own master. But how could he escape them? He thought back to the snippets of Flyte's conversation he'd heard as he drifted into sleep. *I want him. He's mine.*

Flyte's taken me and I've let him . . .

They passed labourers working in the fields, but Reuben hadn't the nerve to cry out to them for help. Who'd believe my story? he wondered. And anyway, they'd only take me back to Birtwell Priory and I can't go back there, not now. Better to let them carry me as far away as possible and then I'll make a run for it.

They travelled all day, along muddy, rutted lanes,

through sleepy hamlets and past lonely houses, across grassy pastures and through dense woods. At last, as the light was fading, Flyte drove the wobbling, creaking wagon across an open meadow to a spot beneath three large, leafless oak trees.

'Camp here tonight,' he said. 'Baggs, show him what's needed to be done.'

Flyte climbed down from the wagon and wandered around their site, smoking his pipe. He didn't appear to look at Reuben, but Reuben was sure that Flyte was aware of every movement he made.

The last hamlet they'd passed was miles back. They hadn't seen a farm for over an hour. He realised escaping wasn't going to be as easy as he'd imagined. Anyway, I haven't the guts to try to run, he thought. Not yet. So he was doing what they asked him to do, gathering wood, building and lighting a fire.

' 'Tis a good spot,' Flyte grunted, looking round. 'Miles from anywhere.'

Baggs, sitting cross-legged on a leather mat on the grass, was skinning a rabbit. He tossed one of its paws at Reuben's head. 'That's for good luck, that is,' he snorted. 'Keep a rabbit's paw around your neck and you'll run faster. It's a fact. You might need that!'

'Don't need to run faster,' said Reuben.

'You might, Skinny Boy, with me after you . . . Didn't your grandmother feed you, ever?'

'She–'

'She fed him bats and rats and stewed pussycat!' said Doctor Flyte. 'Didn't she?'

'No–'

'Poor little Skin-an'-bones,' said Baggs with mock pity.

'Well, you can laugh, I don't think,' said Flyte, heavily. 'Least he had a grandma and a home, which is more than you.'

Baggs bowed his head and chewed his fat bottom lip.

'Baggs ain't got no family,' Flyte went on. 'He was abandoned at birth 'cos he was so ugly – unspeakably ugly for a babe – and put out to a washerwoman, name of old Mother Margaret, who fed him nothing but gruel.'

Baggs shuffled uncomfortably.

'And, she had so many babies to look after, she stuffed them in bags, and hung them around the cottage on pegs!' Flyte nudged Baggs with the tip of his boot. 'That's why we call you Baggs, ain't it? 'Cos you were brought up in one!'

'I swear I do have a ma and a pa,' said Baggs in a voice quivering with emotion. 'I swear they lost me or something, and I swear–'

'Shut up, Baggs. You don't have no one, nor nothing.'

'I do,' whispered Baggs in such a small voice only Reuben heard him. 'I know I do.'

Reuben turned his attention to cutting up the carrots and turnips for the rabbit stew. It was a relief to be off the swaying wagon. He was feeling stronger, his mind working, plans forming.

If I were to run for it, where would I go? he thought. Back to Longford? That was a scary idea. It was so big and noisy. Where then? He'd heard how villages were not allowing folk from other places in. It was hard enough for the parish to care for their own poor without new ones adding an extra burden. He'd never get an apprenticeship, which other boys of his age might do, because he had no family, no letters of recommendation. He was no one. Nothing.

Maybe I could find the village Granny told me about, where her cousin lived. What was it called? Oh, what a long time ago all that seemed now.

He sank into a trance, staring into the bubbling stew as he stirred it, thinking of his grandmother.

'Dreaming?'

Reuben jumped so sharply he almost pitched headlong into the fire.

It was Flyte. Flyte's breath was on his neck as he pressed his hard hand onto Reuben's shoulder, squeezing his bones as if he wanted to crack them.

'She's gone, Reuben,' he said. It sounded almost kind and Reuben, taken off guard, felt his eyes filling with tears. He glanced up and met Flyte's dark, still eyes but there was only an emptiness there.

In a toneless voice, Flyte went on: 'The Devil has

taken her back, boy. But perhaps her soul is still lingering . . . hmm?'

Reuben stirred the pot again.

'Is that it, Reuben? Is she with you? Whispering spells and incantations? Curses to use on us?'

'No, no!'

Reuben wiped his eyes and slunk around the camp fire away from Flyte. He sat down on a stone beside the horse. Nellie was munching her food and blowing into her bag of oats and the sound was comforting. When the tears welled up in his eyes again, he went on staring at the flames, never blinking, letting them run down his dirty cheeks, hoping that if he didn't sniff or wipe them away, Flyte wouldn't notice and Baggs wouldn't mock.

He wanted to think about his grandmother and his other life. He wanted to go back to her, just for a few minutes, just to remember . . . He shut his eyes, shut out Flyte and Baggs, and let the heat from the camp fire become the heat from the summer sunshine on his cheeks; the smell of the stew, one cooked by Granny at her hearth. He was back at Pleck Cottage.

5
Pleck Cottage

The scents and sounds of the garden slipped into Reuben's mind as if through an open window. He licked his lips, thought he tasted honey; golden, garden honey . . .

The garden had been full of aromatic flowers and herbs, cabbages and parsnips and potatoes, all mixed together. They had three ancient beehives woven from willow and mud. Whenever there was a birth or death in the village, Granny and Reuben would go and whisper the news to the bees. Inside the hives, the humming and wing-scuttling noises rose with excitement at his grandmother's voice and Reuben, putting his hand on the hive, could feel the burst of activity and honey-making inside.

Sarah Mearbeck. *Witch. Sorceress. Devil's whore!*

Reuben had tried to get his grandmother to attend the sewing circle or the Tuesday prayer meeting, even the weekly Bible readings, but she only shook her head and instead took herself off into the woods, gathering toadstools and searching out rare herbs. She would never fit in.

Reuben's mother and father had died when he was

one year old and he'd been cared for by a woman who fostered unwanted and orphaned children. When he was small he'd pestered his grandmother again and again to hear the story of her going to find him amongst all the other babies and bring him back to Birtwell Priory to be with her. How she'd recognised him straight away. How he'd stopped crying the moment she'd picked him up. How she'd loved him. And he'd loved her and the villagers used to love her too, or respect her, but now there was all this hostility . . .

Annie Purseglove hired Reuben's grandmother to deliver her daughter Molly's first baby. Everyone for miles around knew Granny Mearbeck was skilled at midwifery. Even a fine young lady at Willsbridge had employed Granny and paid her well when the fine lady gave birth to a chubby baby boy and they were both fit and well.

The Purseglovesʼ cottage was buzzing with activity. Apart from Annie and her daughter upstairs in bed, there was Meg Silver and Elsie Turnbull too, scurrying about like anxious mice, boiling water, ripping up linen, sweeping floors and chattering all the while.

Everything had gone well, Reuben had heard from his place out in the garden, everything was splendid except the baby had a birthmark.

'What caused it?' asked Annie. Her eyes were red-rimmed. She sank down onto the stool beside the window and breathed in the clean, fresh air. 'She's a good girl is our Molly. And I took every precaution, you know I did. There was a good block of iron in her bed to ward off witches. We unlatched every window and door for a smooth delivery, which we had . . . So why's she gone and got a baby with a mark like that? Such a lovely boy he is, otherwise. Jed will be so pleased it's a boy. But that mark!'

'Could have been something to do with *her*,' Meg Silver said, nodding towards Sarah who stood a little apart, hands clasped over her apron.

Elsie Turnbull stopped tearing at the linen. 'Sarah Mearbeck was the one who pulled the cord from around its neck! She saved the wee soul. She wouldn't want to curse it, now would she?' she said.

'I would not,' said Reuben's grandmother, quietly, standing stiffly against the wall.

'What's the matter with the baby, Granny?' Reuben asked, creeping back into the cottage from his listening place outside. He glanced nervously towards the narrow staircase at the top of which, Molly and her baby lay.

The small room downstairs felt as if a tight, invisible cobweb of fear was stretched across it that jangled and vibrated as the women spoke. Worse than Molly's cries and screams filling the place, thought Reuben.

'Nothing is wrong with the baby. Many babies are born with pink or red marks,' said Granny Mearbeck, calmly. 'Even little Reuben has a mark on his neck. It's nothing.'

Reuben fingered his neck where the red stain was hidden. Didn't they want the baby to have a mark? Without it, his grandmother might have picked out the wrong baby at the orphan home. They might never have found each other. He thought it was a great piece of luck to carry a mark from birth. Why didn't she tell them they were lucky?

'He *would* have one, wouldn't he?' said Meg, darkly. 'Little imp.'

'If I could be clever enough to make marks appear I'd be a rich woman, Meg.'

'Aye,' agreed Elsie. 'You're just stirring things, Meg. It's malicious talk, that is.'

Reuben saw how tired his grandmother was. Her bonnet was askew, strands of grey hair had escaped. He wanted to take her home and sit her in her big wooden chair by the fire, brew her tea and maybe they'd share a scone together. She'll be fine, he thought, if I can just get her back home, away from these women.

'No, no, it can't be Mistress Mearbeck. It has to be something Molly's done,' wailed Annie. 'It's such a bright mark, on his dear little face!'

'It'll most likely fade,' said Reuben's grandmother. 'They usually do.'

'She did eat a whole mountain of strawberries last

summer,' went on Annie. 'They say such things can cause these stains and it is so pink!'

Elsie nodded. 'Tell Molly to use her own spittle to wash the mark every morning,' she said. 'I know that'll get rid of it. And my sister told me you should lay a flower against it, now what was it? Dandelion or celandine . . .?

Meg Silver, arms folded tightly, looked pointedly at Sarah Mearbeck.

'It's strange that it should be shaped so, though, isn't it?' said Meg, squinting at her. 'I mean, clear as clear, it's a leaping toad, didn't you think? Poor child. Poor wee thing.'

'A *toad?*' said Elsie, shocked. 'I didn't think so!'

'That's the first thing I thought,' said Meg, with a little crooked smile. Slowly she shook her head. 'Her first baby, marked with the Devil's own. A calamity.'

'It's not shaped like a toad,' said Sarah Mearbeck, sternly. 'That's your imagination. It's a mark of birth. It only looks like a toad to one who's determined to see a toad.'

Annie Purseglove and Elsie exchanged a worried look.

Everyone was scared of toads, Reuben knew, believing them to be evil, poisonous creatures, used by the Devil to carry spells and charms. Toads lived secret lives in dark, damp places; they came and went in mysterious ways and were used for secret things. But Granny and I gathered toadspawn together, Reuben remembered, and watched how the fish in the bubbles turned into four-legged land beasts. I wish I knew how. Toads are magical, yes, but not evil.

Meg Silver stared hard at Sarah. 'You'd better watch your step, old woman,' she hissed. 'You delivered that baby. You might have put that mark on it, just out of spite. Who's to say you didn't? After all, look at Master Rufus from Holme Farm. Paralysed. Legs soft as jelly and who's to blame for that, eh?'

Crackle! Spit! The tension in the room snapped and sparked.

'Let's go home, Granny,' Reuben said, holding out his hand to her.

Sarah pulled her shawl around her shoulders. 'Yes, my lamb, we're going.' She turned to Annie. 'Annie, you know I would never hurt a soul. Your Molly has a fine, healthy boy and you should be glad. The mark looks more like a strawberry than a toad. Meg's a suspicious woman and–' She turned to Meg Silver. 'Why must you try and make things difficult for me, Meg? If you want someone to blame for Master Rufus's legs, then blame Doctor Proctor who was so drunk he couldn't recognise a broken spine when he saw one!'

'Oh! Listen to her! Blame the doctor, would you? You're so grand and mighty you know better than a gentleman? Well, I hope you all heard that?'

'What is it that you want, Meg?' Sarah implored.

'Why? What? *Me?* I've never meant anything discourteous or offensive,' said Meg, stretching her neck like an angry tortoise. 'I know what I know, that's all.'

With dignity, Sarah straightened the white cloth around her head, tied bows in the laces of her jacket and smoothed her apron.

'I think Molly will do very well, Annie,' she said. 'Let her drink the camomile tea whenever she's thirsty. I hope the baby feeds well. Good day to you.'

They went out.

As soon as they were out of view of the cottage, Granny Mearbeck stooped, as if she carried a heavy burden. How frail and diminished she looks, Reuben thought.

He took her hand and swung it gently as they walked home.

'Is that bad, Granny, to have a toad mark on your face?' he asked, though he knew the answer. 'I've got a birthmark, though I'm glad it's not on my face and it's only a little circle . . . And the baby's a boy, isn't it? They did want a boy.'

'A boy like you, Reuben. God has blessed them. The mark didn't look like a toad, but I suppose the rest of the village will think it does. Suspicious fools. Who else can they blame if the baby's not perfect? Themselves? Why do some babies come out so plump and well and others feeble and hardly holding on to life? Who knows? There'll be fewer calls for me as their midwife, once Meg Silver's spread her tale. And we need the money, Reuben, you know we do.'

Reuben pondered on her words. 'When I grow up and I'm a real doctor I'll find out why babies come out so differently,' he said. 'There seems to be a reason for nearly everything, if you know where to look for it.'

'I'm sure you're right, dear, clever boy.' She squeezed his hand.

'But why does Meg torment you?' Reuben went on.

'I don't know . . .' She sighed. 'Well, because it makes her feel cleaner and closer to God, maybe. She likes her Bible. They're all suspicious of what they don't understand, and you know how people feel about witchcraft. Mention the word "witch" and they all start trembling.'

'But why doesn't she like *you*?'

'Because I'm not the same as them. Even though I've lived here for years, I'm still an outsider. I don't mix. And I'm old . . . and I'm ugly.'

'You're not!' Reuben glanced up at his grandmother's profile. Ugly? What was ugly? She had a few whiskers on her chin. She was wrinkled and brown-skinned like a withered apple but her eyes were bright and beady like wet pebbles. She was perfect.

'Meg's ugly and she'll be old too, one day! I despise her!'

'Hush, hush, Reuben.'

'I hate her.'

'Don't say that. I don't want you saying that! You know this village! If she's taken ill, they'll say it's because I've put a curse on her.'

'I wish I *could* put a curse on her.'

'Hush.' His grandmother glanced round anxiously. She pulled him to her. 'Be careful what you say, Reuben. Please. There's been bad feeling against me ever since Master Rufus fell off his horse. And this birthmark on the baby won't help.'

'I'll look after you, Granny. I won't let them say you did anything. I'm strong, you know, even though I'm stick-thin.' He grinned up at her. 'You must teach me all the things you know, then I'll be able to help sick folk, too. I know a lot already, don't I?'

'You do. Ah, Reuben, dear boy, what would I do without you?'

Pleck Cottage. Home. As Reuben pushed open the heavy door, relief flooded through him. It was so grand to be home! The scent from the drying herbs and roots hanging over the fire was sweet and comforting. Even the sight of the clean rushes on the floor and his grandmother's chair, her green apron and pewter mug beside the hearth, made his heart swell with love and pride.

He went straight to put some water in the black kettle and heat it on the fire.

'Hot drink, Granny?'

'Yes, my darling.'

She did not sit down in her customary chair but on the edge of her truckle bed in the far corner. She rubbed her forehead. 'I'll take a drop of honey in it too. My head hurts so.'

'Headache? I know,' said Reuben, with forced brightness. 'Feverfew? And maybe rye? Willow bark?'

'Good boy,' she lifted her head slowly and smiled at him. 'You'd make a fine doctor, if you were a gentleman's son.'

'Oh, yes, I'd like to be a doctor, though I know it's only a dream.' Reuben busied himself making the brew, but out of the corner of his eye he was alarmed to see how his granny sat slumped on the bed as if suddenly her bones didn't support her.

'There isn't any feverfew down here. I'll go fetch some,' he told her.

He climbed the wooden ladder up to his sleeping place in the space below the thatch. It was very dark; the air was rich and thick from the closeness of the thatch and the bundles of drying herbs that hung from the beams. Some of the herbs were bagged in brown paper, others were tied in bundles. At night, as they twisted and spun in the warm air currents, Reuben fancied they were dancing ladies having fun at a May fair.

He took some feverfew down and added it to Sarah's

pewter mug. 'Here, Granny, drink this,' he urged her.

She was lying down now, looking so old and so small. Tears sprang to his eyes. Oh, I'll do for Meg Silver, he vowed, if she hurts my granny!

'Sip this, here, take some,' he urged her. He pulled her up and made her drink. 'That's it, that's good.'

He drew his stool up beside her bed.

'Sing to me, lamb,' she whispered.

Reuben sang very quietly.

'There were three ravens sat on a tree,
Down a down, hey down, hey down,
They were as black as black might be,
With a downnnnnn . . .'

It was the song she had sung to him when he was little, and couldn't settle. He wasn't sure what it was about, except that it had birds and dogs in it and a knight, and he liked all those things so he liked the song. He watched her until she slept, noting the exact moment when her fingers released their hold on the covers and her face softened. The room grew very still and quiet. Outside, men were still working in the fields and their voices were loud in the motionless air. A dog barked.

Darkness slowly descended, the noises ceased outside. The fire crackling in the hearth was the only sound, the only moving thing.

This is what it would be like if she were to die, Reuben

realised. He'd never imagined it before, but he'd be totally alone. He went cold all over, the vastness of the hostile world outside suddenly seeming to crowd around the cottage walls.

'Granny?'

A smile, just a little tug at the corner of her mouth, animated her sleeping face and Reuben went on talking to her, hoping she could somehow hear him.

'I love the summer, don't you? The sun shining in through our little window when the shutters are back?' he said. 'The bees buzz in from the garden and we have to send them back with a word of warning. There's always a blackbird in the thorn tree, isn't there? Boys out in the meadow throwing stones into the brook. And you and me, Granny, safe as . . .' He stopped; swallowed the lump in his throat.

'You wished you'd gone to school, didn't you, Granny?' he began again. 'As if girls could learn the ways of clever gentlemen! I remember you wishing for money for books when I wanted money for a hoop or a good blade. Books. Granny and her papers and ideas. Books of ideas, what a notion! Remember you laughed at me and I laughed at you and wrapped my arms around you. I was nearly as tall as you then. What do we want ideas for? I asked you and you said something about not making do with what we're told. About ideas being new thoughts.

'I had to stop hugging you because you scared me. You

told me how you'd given John Samuel a potion of borage, clary, willow bark and rue when he was sick, how his fever went down. You said that was your very own idea. You were so pleased with yourself, dear Granny. But when you went on talking about discovering how it worked and why it worked, I got scared. I felt the shivers up my back, Granny. It was a warning, but you went on about how in London they cut up dead people, looking inside to see their veins, their heart, their liver and you called it science, when all around our neighbours call it Devil's work and they are cleverer and better learned than us . . . well, some of them.'

Reuben stroked the thin, brown skin on the back of his grandmother's hand where the veins were raised and showing blue and purple. He marvelled at it, at what was going on inside that hand at that very moment, what pumping and pushing and movement that the eye couldn't see.

'Granny, Granny, dearest, we must not always speak what we feel. You told me that yourself. You said be true to yourself, but be careful and know when to keep silent.

'But have we been been careful enough?'

6
The Travelling Medicine Man

'Is that stew ready yet, you bag of bones?'

Reuben blinked at Baggs in surprise, looking around for his grandmother, then quickly fell to stirring the stew.

'Yes. Yes, I think it is.' He peered into the pot, keeping his face averted.

'Good. Doctor! It's ready!'

Reuben's hands were trembling. He sniffed the air, sniffed beyond the stew, sure he could smell his grandmother, as if she'd just vacated the seat beside him, leaving the scent of lavender in the air around him.

Doctor Flyte settled on an upturned box beside them and took the dish that Baggs handed to him, resting it on his sharp knees. He began to eat silently and purposefully, as if this might be his last meal for some time.

'Well, Skinny,' said Baggs, 'not bad. Though you stirred it to kingdom come and back.'

Reuben stared at his plate, pushing the stuff round with a crust of bread.

'Cat got your tongue?' said Baggs.

'Ah, but he's thinking plenty, Baggs – about leaving, I shouldn't wonder, ain't you?' Flyte said, not looking at anything in particular. 'Forget Pleck Cottage, boy, this is your life now.'

Reuben jumped at the mention of his old home. He glanced quickly up at Doctor Flyte, who turned and smiled back at him with his eyes just not meeting his, as if there was something rather comical sitting on Reuben's shoulder.

How did Flyte know where he lived?

Reuben turned away, confused. Picking him up on the road had not been a coincidence, then. No, of course, that was why Flyte had said what he had in the inn: he wanted Reuben.

Unable to look back at Flyte, Reuben stared round at the dark, shadowy trees.

And had another shock.

Sitting halfway up the hill, lit by the yellowy light of the fire, was the shaggy dog he'd seen in the barn that morning.

'It's that dog from Longford!' he blurted out.

The other two looked round towards it.

'Can't be,' growled Flyte.

'What's that cur doing following us?' snapped Baggs, hurling a stick at it.

'Don't hurt it,' begged Reuben.

But the dog only rose unhurriedly, took several

dignified steps to one side and then sat down again, staring.

'Why not?' said Baggs. 'It's just a mutt. Fancy a dog-skin jacket? That'd keep you warm, Skinny.' He pretended to reach for his knife.

'No! No, I don't,' said Reuben. 'It's the dog from the inn. I was just thinking about William, I mean, he'll be sad without it.'

'Sad without a dog? What are you blathering about?' said Baggs.

Reuben ignored him. He felt a little bubble of pleasure rise inside him. The dog had followed them. Followed *him*! Something special *had* passed between them that morning.

'It's walked an awful long way,' said Reuben, quietly.

He had a rabbit bone in his hand and there were some very dry crusts of bread left. He thought about throwing them up to the dog.

'Don't you go tempting that animal near,' said Flyte, eyeing him. 'I don't like dogs. If it comes close *I'll* skin it alive, never mind waiting on Baggs to do it.'

Reuben didn't say anything more.

I'll look after you, he told the dog silently. You stay with me. You can be my friend. When they're not watching, we'll run away together. You and me.

'Did she teach you some spells then?' asked Flyte, suddenly.

'What? Who?'

'You know who I mean.' Flyte sucked the last strands of flesh from a small bone, then waved it at him. 'Well, did she?'

It took Reuben a few moments to realise Flyte meant his grandmother. He didn't know whether to say yes or no. Did Flyte believe his granny had been a witch? Reuben stared into the darkness.

Flyte threw the bone into the fire. 'Reuben?'

'Yes,' Reuben said. 'She was very clever. She taught me many things.'

'Magic? Witchcraft?' This time Flyte was staring up towards the dog. 'Curses? How to put the evil eye on someone? Incantations that could cripple and maim?'

Reuben shook his head fiercely. 'There's no such thing,' he said. 'She never did hurt to anyone, nor wish them ill. She had learning about herbs and things, that was all.'

Flyte's lips curled in a comical pout and he nodded his head slowly as if he was thinking, but Reuben could see Flyte was as suspicious as all the others and didn't believe him.

'You're holding out on us,' said Flyte, 'but we'll make you tell – in the end. Away with you. Go on. Go get some water. Make yourself useful.'

Reuben got to his feet and took one of the dull, flickering lanterns down to the river. He set the light down and plunged the bucket into the icy water. When he turned round, the dog was there.

'Dog! You've come!' Reuben held out the bone and the bread that he'd slipped into his pocket.

She was a bitch, with large, soft brown eyes that were studying him with such intensity that Reuben felt again that the dog was claiming him in some way.

'I'm Reuben,' he whispered. 'What's your name? Good dog, come closer, come!' He offered the food, but the dog wouldn't come any nearer. She wagged her tail gently, encouragingly. 'You understand, don't you? You're my friend. You'll help. Will you come with me? We'll go in the night,' he told her. 'I'm not staying here any longer. I *hate* them.'

And, replacing the dull apathy he'd felt up until now, a real, burning hatred began to spit and spark inside him. What right had they to hold him? To say his grandmother was a witch? To believe he could work spells?

'They can't make me stay. They can't keep me!' he told the dog. 'But I must go back now. Stay close!'

Later, Flyte and Baggs played cards on an upturned box beside the camp fire. Reuben sat a little apart, watching.

Baggs cheated at the game. Reuben saw him slipping cards onto his lap. But he never won. He was cheating to lose.

'Me again!' Flyte said, gathering in the cards. 'You're unlucky at cards, Baggs, just like you're unlucky in life. Jinxed.'

Baggs turned and glowered at Reuben. 'And you can hold your gulsh!' he said.

'I never said a word!'

'Good.'

Reuben hunched himself inside the new cloak, smouldering with emotion. Blockheads, they are, he thought. Bullies and blockheads. I'll show them. When they're snoring and dead to the world from drink, I'll creep off and escape. The night's so black, they'll never follow me. This cloak will keep me snug – no, no cloak, that would be stealing. Shame, but it'll have to be left. Can't give them any reason for chasing after me. I'll go as I am and like it.

He stared at the spot where he'd seen the dog, praying she was still there, waiting. She'll come. She'll be my friend.

When Baggs and Flyte fell into a dispute about the cards, and were distracted, he slipped more crusts and an apple into his pocket, smiling at his own duplicity.

'Time to bed down,' said Flyte, at last. He tapped out the ashes from his pipe. 'I've a mattress in the wagon. You and Baggs sleep underneath.'

'Underneath the wagon?' said Reuben.

'That's what I said.'

'But it's so cold!'

'Well, cuddle up close to Baggs and you'll be snug as a couple of bugs down there,' said Flyte, chuckling.

Baggs lay out his thin, straw mattress for himself and an old rug for Reuben beneath the wagon. Reuben wrapped himself in his cloak and lay down nervously.

'Don't move, now,' warned Baggs as they settled down. 'I've trained myself to wake up at the smallest of movements. Guarding the doctor, see. You move, I wake, you're in trouble.'

'Why are you guarding him?'

Reuben felt Baggs hold his breath while he searched for the words. 'He's my master,' he said at last. 'It's not on paper, not like a real apprenticeship, but that's what it is. He looks after me, I look after him. It's an arrangement, like, and he needs me.'

Reuben didn't reply. Flyte cares nothing for you, Baggs, he thought. He treats Nellie better than you, but have your dreams.

The fire died down. The moon was hidden behind thick clouds. It was so dark without the fire that Reuben couldn't sense any difference with his eyes opened or closed.

He lay still as a log alongside Baggs, waiting for him to fall asleep.

Reuben forced himself to keep awake by singing songs and rhymes in his head until at last he heard Baggs's breathing drop into a steady rhythm, followed by a rattle and grunting noise so he knew he was asleep.

Very, very slowly, he lifted the coverlet and rolled out, taking his boots tucked under his arm. Poised on all fours, he held his breath, listening: no change in Baggs's breathing, no other sounds; so he crawled further out from under the wagon and up to a crouching position. Silence. Easy. He stood up, took three steps towards the river–

'Got you!'

'Oh, Doctor Flyte! I was just–'

'Reuben, you weren't sneaking off, were you?'

A light was struck and a reed candle flared up beside them. It was Baggs.

'The little bugger was stealing your cloak, Doctor!'

'I wasn't stealing!' Reuben tried to shrug the cloak off.

'Not stealing? That's as likely as a fart off a dead man,' said Baggs, chuckling.

'Reuben, Reuben, I am hurt,' said Doctor Flyte in a mock sad voice. 'Stealing from the folk who feed you and care for you? How could you do such a thing?'

The light from Baggs's candle lit half Flyte's face, accentuating its asymmetry. He looked like a devil.

'I wasn't! I was just– You can't keep me h–' cried Reuben.

Suddenly Baggs whacked him in the stomach with his fist.

Whoof! The air flew from him, making a weird, animal noise and he collapsed like a fallen tree, gasping for breath.

Baggs followed his punch with a kick.

'Get back under the wagon and don't move,' said Doctor Flyte. 'You owe me for dinner at the inn. You owe me for last night's lodgings. You owe me for that cloak. You owe me a lot, boy. You go nowhere till your debts are paid, so don't think you can try!'

Weeping and coughing, Reuben crept under the wagon and pulled the cloak over his head. Even so, he could still hear Baggs and Flyte laughing and talking and it was a long time before Baggs crept in alongside him. He gave Reuben a painful pinch before he settled down to sleep himself.

Reuben tried to lie still, but his stomach hurt and his thigh, where Baggs's boot had made contact. Every time he shifted or sniffed, even slightly, Baggs kicked him again.

Reuben's tears did not last long. He soon stopped feeling sorry for himself, and instead, let anger rage around inside. Anger and hatred.

Very well, I'm caught, he admitted to himself. Trapped. But there'll be another day, and then I'll pay them back. I'll be thinking of escape every moment of the day and night – and of revenge. If it were possible, if it were true that I could make magic, I'd make the most horrible curse of all time and send you both to an early, awful, terrible death.

7
Death at the Garden Gate

Reuben sat at Pleck Cottage's single tiny window, looking down the path that led to the village green.

Since November, when Molly Purseglove's baby was born, word had spread about the toad-shaped birthmark; now fewer and fewer people came calling on Granny Mearbeck for remedies.

Reuben wondered if his grandmother had noticed. If she did, she never said anything about it.

He glanced at her as she worked chopping herbs at the table. How tiny she looked, her head bowed, her shoulders crimped in tight and small, like a little dormouse. She'd changed so much since Molly's baby had come. She'd started to mumble under her breath as she stirred her pot at the hearth, to whisper when they were out walking together. Reuben hoped no one had noticed. He tried to block out her mutterings now; they didn't sound right to him.

He turned back to the window.

Master Rufus was never going to walk again, that's what the doctors in Bristol had said, and Reuben knew that the villagers blamed Sarah Mearbeck for that. Poor Master Rufus. He gave me a penny once, Reuben remembered. Who was going to exercise his big chestnut mare now? Master Rufus had looked so brave and dashing, flying over hedges and leaping ditches, he'd been such a favourite with the ladies, but not any longer.

Sarah had told him that even though it was Master Rufus's spine that had broken, his legs were the bits that didn't work. It was all connected: spine, legs, muscle, bone. In his mind's eye, Reuben tried to picture what it could be like inside his own body, with all those parts working together, tightening, flowing, beating, squeezing . . . He tried to imagine his own legs dead and useless. He tucked them under his bottom and waited for them to go numb, then he'd be just like Master Rufus.

Outside, a cold March wind blew at the bare trees. Smoke was snatched from the chimneys and disappeared instantly. It seemed as if the whole world was tossing around outside. As if I were on a galleon, Reuben thought, and the wind in the trees was the roar of the waves. Even the tabby cat on the dead tree stump seemed to think it was a game as she challenged the flickering ivy and dancing leaves to fight.

Black cat. Witch's familiar.

Lucky you're not black or I'd send you away, Reuben told it silently. Pray no one else sees it outside our house. Pray that old trout Meg Silver's not looking this way.

At last, something to look at! The bent, crooked figure

of Old John appeared round the corner of the next cottage. As he turned onto the path, the full force of the wild, angry wind struck him, nearly lifting him off his feet.

Reuben grinned; maybe the old man would be tossed up into the clouds by the blustering wind. Would serve him right. He'd given Reuben and his friend Jack such a whipping for stealing pears from his orchard. Miserable old fool!

Reuben watched the old man battle his way down the muddy path towards Pleck Cottage. Probably on his way to Back Row, the cottages beyond, where his daughter, Elsie Turnbull, lived. The old man's gnarled, twisted fingers clutched at his hat as the wind tugged it.

As Old John hobbled past the cottage, the tabby cat suddenly flew off the wall and – back-arched, claws drawn – it pounced on something on the ground.

Startled, Old John stopped. His body jolted upright, rigid as a poker. His hands flew to his chest, grabbing at the cloth. He crumpled, falling heavily to the ground.

'Granny!' Reuben jumped up, but his numb legs buckled under him. 'Ow, my legs! Granny! Come quick!'

He yanked the cottage door open and hobbled, limped and hopped down the garden path to Old John.

He didn't see Meg Silver, staring out through her window opposite, watching.

'What is it?' Sarah called, hurrying behind him, gathering up her long skirts.

When she saw the fallen body of Old John she looked up and down the path anxiously. 'Oh, no,' she said softly, holding her apron to her mouth. 'No.'

'What happened to him?' Reuben called, rubbing his own legs back to life. 'I saw him go down! The cat jumped out and frightened him. I saw it.'

'It's his heart, I think,' said Sarah. 'Go for Elsie!'

Reuben ran. His legs were still prickling, but he ran all the way through the tearing wind down to Elsie's cottage and thumped on the door.

'What is it?' Elsie's husband, Tall John, shouted.

'Elsie's dad's been took sick.'

'Where? How? Silly old bugger. What's he done now?'

'He fell down, right outside our gate,' said Reuben, pleased to be able to give such a good account. 'Crumpled like he'd been hit with a hammer.'

He didn't mean to make fun of the old man, but it *had* been a dramatic collapse.

'Is that Reuben?' Elsie was at the door, pulling the laces of her bodice tight and wrapping a shawl around her shoulders.

Children cried from inside the tiny, dark cottage. Reuben could just make out John Turnbull sitting by the fire, smoking a pipe; a puppy dog; a baby on the floor, chewing on a rag.

'My dad, you say? I'm coming,' Elsie called.

Elsie's skirts whipped up in the wind, her long hair was torn out from under her bonnet and slapped against her face, as they battled up the path to Pleck Cottage.

'Is he all right, then? Is your granny looking after him?'

'Yes, she's with him. She said it was his heart.'

'His heart? How'd she know that? What did she do?'

'Nothing,' said Reuben, confused. 'But he went down just like Mistress Grundy. That was her heart, wasn't it?'

Granny Mearbeck was kneeling beside Old John when they got there. His eyes were closed, his grey skin so loose it looked as if it were slipping off his bones. His thin lips, folded back over his toothless gums, were blue; even the tips of his ears were blue. Reuben's grandmother held the old man's hand, bending her head close to his. She looked up at Elsie as they drew near and Reuben got a shock when he saw her face: it was fearful . . . Why?

The hairs on the back of his neck prickled.

'I'm sorry, Elsie,' Sarah Mearbeck said softly.

'Stop! Stop her!' Meg Silver came towards them shouting, stamping and blowing like a plough horse, dragging her husband along with her. 'Stop!' She waved her arms at them. 'Stop!'

'Let go of me, woman,' Henry Silver puffed at her. 'Leave me be!' His plump face was red, his shirt laces undone, his thick stockings hung untidily in folds around his hairy shins. 'It's none of our business. Let go!'

Meg ran straight to Elsie, ignoring everyone else.

'Elsie! Elsie!' she cried, clutching the young woman's arm. 'Don't let them touch him! I saw it all. Granny Mearbeck did it. Her and that cat! Her *familiar.*'

'Did what? What happened?' Elsie was kneeling down beside her father's body, patting his chest. 'Dad, Dad! The old chap's not breathing! What happened? What about Sarah, Meg?'

'Granny didn't do anything,' said Reuben, trying to keep his voice steady. 'Don't dare say she did!'

Meg's normally pink face was blazing red with excitement. Her small eyes were scrunched up even smaller. Like a spiteful pig, Reuben thought.

'I saw it all,' said Meg, tugging at Elsie's arm. 'The Devil was in that cat! It leaped so high! It wasn't natural. She must have made it do it. It jumped out at Old John just as he walked by!'

'No,' said Reuben, 'no, it wasn't that. The cat was playing, it pounced on something!'

'You hush, you devil, you!' screeched Meg, spinning around and pointing a trembling finger at him. She could hardly control herself. Gobs of spit flew out of her mouth. Her head wobbled on her plump neck.

'I saw you! Hobbling like the crooked little imp that you are! Why were you staggering like a drunkard, eh?

Why couldn't you walk? Not used to walking on two legs, eh? I know, I know!' She jigged about with excitement. 'It was you, you, changing shape right before my eyes! You take on the form of a cat when nobody's watching, that must be it! That's when you go out around the countryside doing your devilish tricks and putting curses on us all. A cat that can leap as high as a tree and kill an old man!' She held her hand to her heart. 'Oh, oh, it's too terrible!'

'Meg.' Sarah Mearbeck spoke gently, but firmly. 'Hush, that's nonsense, you know it is. Reuben, don't listen. '

'What does she mean, Granny?'

'I know what I saw,' said Meg. 'The boy could hardly walk and he can now. How's that possible, unless it's witchcraft? And where's this mysterious cat, eh? The cat has vanished into the air around us!'

'We must move your father, Elsie,' Sarah said, but Meg wasn't stopping for anything.

'Why else would poor Old John fall right outside *your* cottage? Why else, hmm? Isn't it bad enough that he's been too sick to work this past month? Who did that to him, I wonder? Who was it spoiled his back and stopped his breathing from coming regular? And all because poor Old John – an old, old man – punished naughty boys for stealing his fruit, eh, Reuben? Which was right and proper as it was plain robbery. That's it, isn't it?'

'Hush, woman,' snapped her husband, raising his hand

to silence her. 'What happened exactly, Mistress Mearbeck?' he asked.

'He fell. He collapsed,' said Reuben's grandmother. 'Bring him in before it's too late. I'm so sorry.'

'Sorry!' screamed Meg. 'Yes! You'll be sorry, you'll be very sorry! I saw you that time, I caught you at it. Not done enough damage yet? Not satisfied with marking Molly's baby with your witch's toad – no!' Meg stamped her feet and wrenched at her skirt, splitting the seam. 'You won't get away with this! I'll see that you don't. Always watching us. Always keeping to yourself and making your witch's brews. Well, it's too late for *you*, Sarah Mearbeck.'

'Meg, Meg . . .' Her husband pulled at her to come away.

'He's an old man,' said Elsie, looking from Meg to Sarah. 'He's not been so well. I don't know . . .' Suddenly Elsie cried out in a faint, worried voice: 'Oh, look!'

Something moved at the base of the rotten tree stump.

'There! It is! It's a toad!'

Meg screamed and cackled with triumphant laughter. 'I knew it! I knew it!'

Beneath the hanging ivy, a large brown toad blinked up at them as it shuffled nervously backwards into the shelter of the dead tree.

'Ahh!' Meg screeched. 'You see! Didn't I tell you? She's turned the cat into a toad! Another familiar.

Witches use toads and here it is, proof! Another poor, lowly creature doing her bidding. Witch! Sorceress!'

'I've never given time to these gossips about you till now,' said Elsie to Granny Mearbeck. 'You saved our John's arm when he got a stone dropped on it and it turned bad. You've looked after my babies . . . Sarah, I don't want to believe it, but . . .'

'Then don't,' said Sarah, simply. 'Don't, because it's not true. I can't do magic. I have no malice in me, I swear! I'm just–'

'It's *her* you must not listen to,' spat Meg. 'She killed him! You, Mistress Mearbeck – you and your demons, your mediums and magic! Toads and potions. You did this! Just as well I wear my lucky toad's leg,' she went on, pulling out a small satin bag from her bodice. 'I've been warned. Why d'you think I haven't been harmed, eh? Because I have my toad's leg as protection.'

'Hush, hush,' said Sarah quietly. 'Think of Old John. I may still be able to help him, we should–'

'No, don't let her touch him,' said Meg. 'Elsie, do you see me harmed at all? No! I chopped off the toad's leg and put it safe in here. I buried its body under an alder tree at the full moon. There's more proof for you, don't you see?'

'Elsie?' Sarah looked at her young friend, pleadingly.

'No,' said Elsie, not meeting her eyes. 'Molly's baby does have that mark and Master Rufus, well . . . and now my own dad. No, don't touch him, Mistress Mearbeck. Don't!'

Reuben watched his grandmother back away. She seemed to shrivel, wither and age before his eyes as she tottered back to the cottage door.

'Granny!' he cried, and wrapped his arms around her waist. 'Granny! Don't!'

'That's right, Reuben, you tell her, make her keep back. Don't let her near him,' cried Meg, clutching her satin purse.

'I didn't mean *that*!' he snorted crossly. 'You're mad! I was never a toad. The cat was playing. The toad is just a toad! Look!'

He picked up a stick and waved it in front of the creature.

The toad's yellow eyes seemed to flash like precious jewels. It reared up on its hind legs and leaped towards the stick, its wide mouth gaping and angry. Reuben stepped back, gawping.

'Granny? Why did it do that?'

'See that? See that?' squeaked Meg, flapping at her apron. 'That's no proper toad, that's no ordinary creature, that isn't. Mearbeck's a witch, I've always said. I've seen you muttering and staring.'

'The toad is just worried,' said Sarah, mildly. 'It's all it can do in defence. Leave it alone. Oh, Meg,' said Sarah, quietly. 'Why must you have these imaginings and dark thoughts – you've managed to make my life harder than it needed to be.'

Elsie's husband, Tall John, arrived. He didn't ask anything, but knelt down beside Old John and studied his face.

'Hush your squabbling, women. Come on. Let's get him moved,' he said. 'Here, Henry, help me get him to the cottage.'

Sarah and Reuben went back into Pleck Cottage, bolting the door behind them.

It was dark inside and a relief to be free of the constantly nagging wind tossing their clothes and roaring against their ears.

'Old Meg Silver's a bilious boil,' said Reuben, trying to be light-hearted, staring at his grandmother's shrunken, lined face. Hating it. 'Granny? I said, Meg's just a pustule, isn't she, and she can't hurt us?'

'Come here, Reuben.'

Reuben sat on the low stool beside her and wrapped his arms around her thickly-skirted legs.

'I am not a witch,' she said. 'Not unless a witch is an old woman who helps make people better.'

'I know.'

'I've made people better, haven't I? Better than that fool, Doctor Proctor. Better than old Smithers, the barber-surgeon. And which of us can afford for them to come and visit, hey?'

'What's going to happen, Granny?' Reuben put his small hand on her hand. 'We'll be all right, won't we?'

'Oh, Reuben, don't you understand at all? They think I'm a witch. They'll want to lock me up and . . .'

'And what?'

'You know what they do to witches. They hang them.'

'They wouldn't hang you! Why? How could anyone be scared of you? You're just my granny. I want things to go on the way they are, for ever and ever.'

Sarah stroked his head as she pulled him to her. 'I want that too. I should have been more careful. I thought I *was* careful. Never a cross word to anyone, in case they tripped up afterwards and believed I'd cursed them. Never an angry gesture all these years, but *still* they fear me. It's superstition and ignorance,' she said. 'Ignorance is like a dark ditch of stagnant water which people like Meg Silver have fallen into and can't get out of. Why, Meg's not even struggling, but splashing around in there, happy as a hog! At least you know your letters, Reuben. At least you've got your eyes open, your head ready to learn . . . Remember your lessons and seek the truth, won't you?'

'I will, Granny.'

'Reuben, last summer, that poor old woman who came to the village, all covered in sores, limping and tired? What did they do to her?'

'I don't remember,' lied Reuben.

'You do. She had a wart on her nose, her eyes were cloudy and she talked to the trees, the stones, everything around her. One of Farmer Sneddon's sheep blew up like a balloon and dropped down dead. Meg Silver said she'd seen the old woman gazing over the wall at it, putting a spell on it.'

Reuben's throat tightened. He could remember it very clearly. It appeared in his mind, a brightly-coloured, vivid picture.

It had been late in the day; the shadows were long, striping the grass around the large pond with bars of black. Most of the village had gathered there. Some of the women were begging that they let the old woman go, while the squire, Farmer Elton and others were urging Farmer Sneddon on. Reuben had been told to stay away, but he'd crept out with his friends and watched.

The old woman was tied up like a Christmas goose. Her long, grey hair hung loose around her face. She was weeping, calling out to God to save her. The boys laughed because they didn't know what else to do.

'The men ducked her in the pond until she came up dead, didn't they?' said Sarah, reliving the moment too. 'The poor old biddy. Survive the ducking and you're a witch. Drown and you're innocent. The woman hadn't a chance. Didn't it delight Farmer Sneddon? And weren't the churchwardens pleased? They wouldn't have to find her a place to sleep or money to feed her.'

Reuben suddenly realised what his grandmother was trying to suggest to him. He jumped away from her so that he could look up into her blue eyes.

'No! Not you!'

'They might. Or they might hang me . . .'

'I won't let them!' cried Reuben. 'I won't. Why would they do that to you? You help people! You're . . . you!'

'Dearest . . .'

'Please, Granny, please don't let them do that.'

She gathered him into her arms. 'Whatever happens, Reuben, dear boy, remember, I will always love you. I will always watch over you and keep you safe.'

8
A Day at the Fair

Reuben woke that morning, sensing that something had just left his side.

He lay for a few minutes staring up at the wooden axle and workings on the underside of wagon, realising where he was, remembering what had happened the night before. When he moved, his body hurt from the kicks and punches and from sleeping on the hard earth. It must have been Baggs getting up that had woken him, he thought, and made him suddenly cold.

He sniffed: there was a peculiar smell lingering. A strong aroma, like old food and wet fur, hung around him. Maybe it was Baggs – he was certainly dirty enough.

'Boy! Come here, boy!' Flyte was shouting for him.

Reuben crawled out, stretched his stiff limbs and stood in front of Doctor Flyte. He lowered his head, keeping his eyes down, but inside his heart was bursting with defiance.

'Last night was disappointing,' said Flyte. 'After all I've done for you, boy. Don't ever, ever, try and run away again.' Flyte took Reuben's arms and squeezed them tightly. 'I can be a mean and hard master if I have to, Reuben.' His fingers were like iron, digging into his upper arms as he spoke. 'We saved you and you should be glad of it. Now you pay us back. Go and help Baggs clear up.'

'Yes.'

'Yes, Doctor Flyte.'

'Yes, Doctor Flyte.'

'We're going to market today, working. You're coming too, so mind you behave yourself. Hold your gulsh, not a peep. Don't give me any cause to be angry with you, will you?'

Reuben shook his head.

'Let go of your other life, boy. You belong to us.' Flyte took off his jacket and laid it out on a stone. It was stained and spotted with grease marks and Flyte eyed it critically. 'Hear me, boy?'

Reuben nodded again, then quickly added, 'Yes, Doctor Flyte.'

'I knew you'd understand soon enough,' said Flyte. He reached into the caravan and brought out a small bottle of vinegar. 'This'll get rid of the dirt and the stink. Must look my best for my performance, eh?'

'Yes, Doctor Flyte,' Reuben agreed wearily.

Baggs grinned and cuffed Reuben around the head.

'You belong to us!' he repeated. 'And that means I tell you what to do. So I will. Go get the fire lit and bring up the water. We'll have oatcakes and ham before we go, shan't we, Doctor Flyte?'

'We shall. There's much work ahead of us.'

When Reuben came back with the water and had got the fire going, he found Baggs untying the short laces which held down the covers on the wagon's curved canopy and rolling them up. Beneath were brightly-coloured pictures of a man not unlike Doctor Flyte, and some writing.

'That's fine, ain't it?' said Baggs. 'Don't suppose you know the meaning of them words, though, do you?'

Reuben nodded.

'You can read?' Baggs's face fell. 'Well, you little turkey-cock, go on then, what does it say?'

'Why don't you read it to me?' said Reuben.

Baggs aimed a fist at Reuben's head, but Reuben dodged out of the way quickly, laughing.

'What's the matter, Baggs, don't know your letters, is that it?' said Reuben, scornfully.

Growling like a bear, Baggs jumped on him and threw him to the ground, squashing the wind out of him and pummelling his head with his fists. 'Shut your gob! Take it back!'

'I'm sorry, I'm sorry!' Reuben yelled. 'I just– Ow! Stop!'

Flyte hauled Baggs off him and threw him against the wagon. Reuben got up slowly, desperate to hold back his tears.

'You fox-faced scumbag!' roared Baggs.

'Reuben, that wasn't kind,' Flyte said, shaking his head. 'It doesn't pay to cross Baggs, I'd have thought you'd have learned that already.'

Baggs grinned and wiped his nose with the cuff of his sleeve. 'Yeah!'

'He's sorely lacking in the composition of his brain,' went on Flyte. 'I suggest you leave him alone.'

Baggs's face took on a sad and pained expession as it slowly dawned on him that Flyte was being cruel, but he quickly covered his hurt by punching Reuben again.

'Yeah,' he added. 'Little turkey cock.'

Reuben sobbed and shook his head. 'I won't tease him again.'

'Read it me, then, and no messing around this time,' said Baggs, breathing hard. 'Know-all.'

Reuben read: '*Doctor Flyte's Fantastic Formula. We aim to please. We aim to ease. Magical toadstones. Potions. Cure-alls.*'

'Very good,' said Doctor Flyte.

'Are you really a doctor?' asked Reuben. 'I mean, did you study in Latin and everything?'

Flyte nodded.

'But why do you keep the writing covered over?' asked Reuben. 'It looks much nicer than the cloth.'

Baggs laughed and cuffed Reuben's ear so fiercely his head rang. 'You'll work that one out soon,' he said, mysteriously.

* * *

It was several hours' ride to Clodbury.

Reuben suffered the uncomfortable journey in silence, looking ahead at the muddy track, letting the clanking and clunking of the rolling wheels lull him into a sort of dream, only the bitter smell of vinegar from Flyte's jacket occasionally jarring him awake. He wondered where they were going and what was going to happen to him and he almost didn't care; he felt so sore from Baggs's beating, and so lonely.

But Reuben was alert enough to notice that when the wagon swung left along the road – following the track the milestone claimed led to Clodbury – there was something slinking along the road behind them.

The dog! It was the dog!

He was so excited he almost cried out, but bit back the words before he uttered a sound. They mustn't see her! They'd try and scare her away. So Reuben never looked back, but in his mind's eye, he pictured the shaggy dog as she sloped along behind them, her long, lanky legs effortlessly covering the miles. His faithful shadow. *Shadow*. Yes, that's what he'd call her. He could bear anything while his Shadow was with him. He smiled and sat up a little and found his limbs didn't hurt so much.

Half a mile from Clodbury village, the track ran

straight, the view was unimpeded, and Reuben saw they were approaching something terrible. He felt the blood rush to his cheeks. Bile crept up from his stomach and burned his mouth.

Outlined against the almost white sky, a man's body hung black and tattered from a crudely made gallows. Even from this distance, Reuben was sure he could see the dead body swing back and forth in the wind and hear the creak of the rope. He closed his eyes, determined not to open them until they'd gone by.

'It's a two-legged tree!' said Baggs.

Flyte chortled. 'Look there,' said Doctor Flyte lightly, as if he was pointing out a pretty flower or noble tree. 'A thief of the highways. Do look, Reuben, boy. Hanged by the neck, he is. See how the crows have pecked out his eyes? They say the eyeball is a tasty morsel. Perhaps I'll ask for one, next time we dine at The Longford Arms?'

He reined Nellie to a standstill and the wagon came to a halt. Nellie snorted with disgust at the smell, rolled her eyes and tossed her mane.

'Have a look,' Flyte said, nudging Reuben. 'A painful, horrible death, is hanging. But better than burning. Imagine your skin melting off your bones while you watch! The heat! Ow! The searing pain!' He laughed, smacking Reuben on the knee so smartly the flesh stung. 'Open your eyes or I'll whip you!'

Reuben opened his eyes. He found himself staring at a pair of old boots with misshapen square toes. The leather was creased and scuffed. The toes pointed downwards as if their owner was still desperately trying to reach the ground. They circled slowly, round and round. Reuben glimpsed the yellowing, sagging dead flesh of the man's shins.

'Did *she* look like that, eh, boy? Did she go quick or slow, giving her familiars time to leap from her mouth as she died?' Doctor Flyte whispered close to Reuben's ear. 'Did they come to you with their secrets? What do you know? Tell me!'

'Nothing,' Reuben gasped. 'Don't . . .'

'I don't believe you,' said Flyte. He slapped the reins over Nellie's back and she gladly lurched into action. 'But I can wait,' added Flyte. 'Plenty of time.'

Reuben stared at Nellie's broad back and dark mane as it rose and fell. Far away he heard a dog barking and hoped it was his Shadow dog.

They trundled slowly towards the village. As the first few cottages on the edge of Clodbury came into view, Baggs suddenly said, 'This'll do. I'll get out here.'

He took a small leather bag from behind the seat and jumped down, pulling his crumpled hat low.

'Meet you later,' Baggs called with a wave, then ambled off down the road, shoulders hunched, whistling.

'Get on, Nellie!' Flyte flicked her rump. 'No questions?' he asked Reuben.

Reuben shook his head. He did wonder where Baggs was going, but if they wanted his questions, he wouldn't give them.

Clodbury Fair was in full swing. There were stalls selling food, old clothes, linen, books. Three men were wearing red and green costumes, tumbling and jumping through the square. Children ran screaming and shouting through the crowds. Some of them cheered and called to Doctor Flyte when they saw him.

Reuben thought immediately of escape. Surely here he'd get a chance. But as Flyte guided Nellie through the crowds, he leaned down to whisper into Reuben's ear: 'Don't even think about it, Reuben. I'll be watching you every minute. Even when you think I'm not, I will be. Not a word. I don't want to have to call you a liar in front of all these folk. Or let Baggs give you another beating . . .'

Reuben said nothing.

Beside the square, between an oak tree and a low wall, Doctor Flyte found a patch of thin grass for Nellie to munch and space for the wagon. He jumped down, hobbled the horse then turned back to Reuben.

'Come on!' snapped Flyte. 'Come here!'

'Yes,' muttered Reuben, going to him quickly.

Flyte was so much taller than him, so much broader, larger, louder; Reuben felt like a twig beside him, about to be snapped and broken. Flyte's hard eyes glistened brilliantly like chips of stone as he gripped Reuben's arm.

'Yes, Mister Flyte?' whispered Reuben.

'No, no, no, Reuben!' His hands snatched at Reuben's clothes, plucking at the shirt collar, hovering around his birthmark. 'Haven't I told you? Told you and told you? *Doctor* Flyte, *DOCTOR!*' He put his twitching, clutching hands behind his back and leaned down, his face inches from Reuben's. 'You understand, boy?'

'Yes, sir. Doctor.'

'Yes. You do. You do.' He straightened up, unclenched his fists. 'Well then, go, let the back down. Get the bottles out. Mind you don't break anything!'

Reuben breathed out at last. He ran to do as he was told.

Bottles? Of medicine, he supposed. Reuben had seen last night how the rear of the wagon opened to make a small platform. He scrambled round to the back of the vehicle and unlatched it now, as Baggs had done before. Inside, behind the curtain, he found the boxes of medicine. Carefully, he took the tiny, green glass bottles from their cradles of hay, and stood them in neat rows on a small trestle table. His fingers were shaking so much he thought he would surely drop something.

'What you got there?' asked a girl with big brown eyes. 'Something pretty?'

Reuben shook his head at her, wished her away.

'Bit young to be a tooth-puller, aren't you?' said another voice in his ear.

'What you selling?' said a third voice.

Reuben ignored them all and nodded his head towards Doctor Flyte.

'Demonstration in five minutes!' cried the doctor. 'Tell your friends. Demonstration in five minutes! Come and see Doctor Flyte's wonderful formula!'

Reuben felt a tingle of excitement run up and down his spine. He was sure something exciting was about to happen. What did this formula do? And where was Baggs?

'Ring this!' snapped Flyte, pressing a little hand-bell at him. 'Go on!'

Nervously, Reuben stepped on to the platform and rang the bell.

'Louder!'

Clang! Clang! It was dreadful the way everyone turned and looked at him. Reuben felt the blood rush to his cheeks. Someone might recognise him. There might be someone from his village! He tucked his chin into his collar, trying to hide.

Doctor Flyte began shouting and calling, and more and more people came over to see what was going on. Within minutes, a crowd had collected at the back of the wagon, peering up at Reuben and Doctor Flyte.

'Gather round! Gather round! I am the famous Doctor

Flyte, maker and purveyor of Flyte's Fantastic Formula! Fabled throughout the lanes and byways of this country. Doctor Flyte, the Miraculous Man of Medicine. With you for one afternoon only!'

A curtain hung beside Reuben, separating the platform from the interior of the wagon. Reuben slipped behind it. From here he could just see Flyte's profile, and marvelled, with a sort of wonderful terror, at his face: his broken, twisted nose hooked over his almost lipless mouth. His flashing, dark eyes.

'I search out the ill, the weak and the weary and I make them well again!' cried Flyte. 'My miraculous, wonderful formula, is all you need for a better life!'

Flyte's arched eyebrows jigged erratically above his dark eyes as he spoke. He was awesome!

By now a good crowd had gathered. They'd seen the jugglers and the tooth-puller. They'd bought their vegetables, geese, eggs and cheese – now they wanted to be entertained and Flyte looked like the man to do it.

He raised both arms, demanding quiet.

'Well, you look a fine bunch,' he said, smiling down at them. 'I shall go home poor, for it doesn't appear that anyone here is in need of my Fantastic Formula. Bursting with health you are. Is there no one sick? No one here who might wish to avail themselves of Flyte's medicines while they have the chance? I shall be gone again before you can blink. Is there a good housewife who needs a tonic? A lad with insidious indigestion? Black bile in the system? An old man with bucolic palpitations?'

There were cries from the crowd:

'Over here!'

'Our Timothy's got that!'

'You, mistress!' Flyte turned his dark, intense look on a large woman clutching a threadbare shawl around her shoulders. She had deep shadows beneath her eyes and squinted, as if the light was too bright. She needs spectacles, thought Reuben, she can hardly see. Old Mistress Hall in Birtwell Priory had been the same.

'What ails you, mistress? Is it the wambling trot? The quavering kidneys? I can cure them all with my Fantastic Formula!' He waved one of the little green bottles at them.

'Nothing wrong with me,' the woman laughed.

'I need only to touch your flesh and it will reveal your weaknesses,' said Flyte, catching her large hand in his and trapping her like a fly in a web. 'Ah,' he said, pressing her fingers, turning her hand and rubbing her palm, and all the time staring into her pale face. 'It's your eyes, isn't it?'

'Oh! Devil's work!' She snatched her hand away. 'My eyes indeed! Let me go!' She pushed her way back through the crowd, which parted to let her through, like a wave, then oozed forward again, anxious to hear more.

How *had* he known what was wrong with the woman?

They wondered. Was he a wizard? A magician? A truly clever doctor?

'What's wrong with me then?' said a thin man offering his hand to Flyte. 'Go on, Doctor, what's wrong with me?'

Flyte tilted his tall hat to the back of his head and took the man's hand in his, turning it over, squeezing it and examining his nails closely.

Doctor Flyte stared intently at the man. 'Splintering of the spleen!' he pronounced. 'A strange pain here, and here?' He pointed to his own stomach and side. 'Sometimes in the back, too? These vapours pass from the right side where the liver is situated, to the left side where the heart is and down to the spleen.'

'Oy! That's the truth, that is! That's my pain all right.' The man looked surprised. 'Who told you?'

The crowd laughed.

'It's the spleen,' said Flyte. 'That, and the encrustations in the liver. Too much ale, my friend. Too many women and lusty thoughts!'

The audience cheered.

'What about me?' croaked a thin, old man with long, grey hair, hobbling towards Flyte, holding a hand against the small of his back. 'Can you guess what ails me?'

'Guess? I don't guess, *young* sir, I *know*! It's your spine. Your back is your bother. You have fibulations and fibrous fixations of the spine! Your joints are stiff,' he told him, 'your back is as tight as an iron bar.' Flyte waved a bottle at them. 'My Fantastic Formula will release the build-up of bad matter, which has accumulated on the axis of the bones, and let the good matter circulate. One spoonful, twice a day and you'll be dancing all night!'

'He's right about my back, he is,' sighed the old man.

Flyte didn't press the man to buy his Fantastic Formula; instead he turned to a young mother with a baby in her arms and a small boy beside her. They were dressed in dirty rags. Their bones showed sharply as if they were trying to pierce through their pale skin.

Reuben guessed their problem was lack of food.

'Sir, sir, can you help my boy, George?' the mother asked, pulling her son forward. He was not much more than a skeleton: grey-skinned with big, tragic eyes.

'George. George!' Flyte took the tiny morsel of a child by the hand and hoisted him effortlessly onto the wagon's platform where everyone could see him.

The boy stared listlessly down at his mother.

'A moment, please, while I place my hands on his dear little head,' said Flyte, turning back his shirt cuffs and exposing his wiry, pale forearms. The shirt laces dangled across the boy's face as Flyte lay his long palm over the boy's head, but the boy was so feeble he didn't flick them away. Closing his eyes, Flyte's delicate brows rose and fell with the scientific thoughts that were criss-crossing his brain. 'An infestation,' he murmured, shaking his head. 'Mistress, does this boy eat?'

'Yes, sir, a little; I mean, when he can.'

'He eats, and yet, isn't it true, he is not happy? Not playing and chattering the way a young boy should, at his age?'

'Yes, sir, how did you know, sir? Oh, can you help him? Is it worms? Is that it?'

'Flyte's Formula fixes everything! The boy will be shouting and running after tasting this stuff. Three pennies a bottle and cheap at the price. This elixir contains all manner of rare herbs, spices and chemicals, from as far away as Egypt, Madagascar and the Orient. It is unique. It is marvellous! It will have George here glowing with health in five days. Just one spoonful, once a day and the boy will be fit for anything.'

'Well, three pennies . . .' George's mother shook her head and pulled her little son down. 'Oh, George, my dear, it's *that* expensive . . .'

Reuben wished Flyte would just *give* her the medicine. She needed it and she couldn't pay. He patted his own pockets, but it was useless; there wasn't so much as a farthing in them.

People were clamouring to buy bottles now, and yet Flyte still wasn't pressing them to buy. Coins clinked as purses were emptied: why didn't Flyte sell the stuff to them?

Reluctantly, Reuben admired Flyte – he wasn't going to sell a single bottle until they were all desperate and ready to pay double!

'You sir, you with the hat!' cried Flyte, suddenly.

The crowd strained their necks to see whom Flyte meant. It was a plump-faced youth with a very tall, battered hat. His long, matted hair reached past his shoulders. A black patch hid one eye. His cheeks and chin were white and lumpy.

'Come closer, young sir,' cried Flyte, urging the lad to come up to the wagon. 'Come here. I've got a feeling about you!'

9
Hidden Talents

The youth shuffled up to the front.

'Suppose you're going to tell me there's something amiss with my eye?' said the youth, turning to let everyone see his eye patch.

The crowd laughed.

'No, sir. Something wrong with your *stomach*!' cried Flyte triumphantly.

'I don't believe it!' cried the youth, one hand flying involuntarily to his stomach and clutching it. 'He's right! How do you know that? Can you read my mind? My guts are bad, terrible! Rotten and aching. They keep me awake at night. Can you mend them?'

'I believe I can. Step up here, sir. Be the first to try the quality of my medicine. Tell me,' went on Flyte, picking up a bottle of his formula, 'do you have the stone squitchers? The squirts?'

'I do. I think I do! It's agony. Ow, ow, even now, the pains are so bad.' He buckled and moaned, hideously.

The crowd whispered sympathetically.

'Poor man.'

'Poor dear.'

'Stones are so painful! They burn up me insides and twist me guts.'

'Then you shall be the first to try my fantastic potion,' said Flyte. 'At no charge, sir, if you'll let these good people watch the result.'

The youth was doubled up with agony. He gripped his stomach and groaned. 'It comes on so sudden. Anything, anything, just take the pain away.'

Flyte pulled the cork from a bottle of his mixture and poured some carefully out into a small spoon. The syrup was dark and must have smelled strong because the youth recoiled, making a face.

'Is it safe?'

'Safe as houses.' Flyte approached with the spoon. 'Open your mouth.'

'I'm scared–'

'No need to be scared, this is good medicine. This is the elixir of the gods. It will course through the obdicules and ventricles of your body, slip through the capistilations of your veins and in minutes you will have relief from the pain!'

'But–'

Flyte tipped the spoon into his mouth and the youth swallowed the liquid. He stood there gulping, swallowing, then went very still. His mouth remained crumpled with distaste, his eyes tight shut.

The crowd edged forward, holding their breath, watching . . .

'Why doesn't he move?'

'What's wrong with him?'

'What's in that stuff?'

'Wait just a little while. The extraordinary curative nature of my elixir will show itself in just a moment . . .'

Suddenly the youth leaped in the air. The audience jumped back in alarm, cries of surprise bursting from them.

'Ayeeo!' cried the youth. A big grin lit up his ugly face. 'It's gone. It's gone. The stone's vanished!'

'Deconstructed, dissolved and done away with!' said Doctor Flyte, smugly. He rubbed his hands together gleefully, grinning at the audience.

'I don't feel that heavy stone in my gut. I'm as light as a feather. I'm lighter than air. My insides are free!' said the youth.

The crowd cheered and hooted.

'The cramp, the stitch, the squirt, the itch! I cure them all!' cried Flyte. He flung back the curtain and hissed at Reuben: 'Get out and get their money.'

Reuben scuttled out, feeling like a spider. Without a word, he took the pennies thrust at him and in exchange, handed over the small, green bottles of potion. Why was there something familiar about the youth? Had Reuben seen him before? Was he perhaps from Birtwell Priory?

And at the back of Reuben's mind was a nagging worry. What could Doctor Flyte have put in his formula to have such a wonderful effect? Even his grandmother's potions weren't as successful as that! Whatever it was, it was good and strong. He smiled as he handed a bottle to little George's mother. I hope it works, he thought, taking their money.

Something else was worrying him too. The miraculously cured youth with the eye patch had miraculously disappeared.

Reuben sold bottles until there was no one else to sell them to. Looking round, he saw the square was emptying – only a few villagers lingered, picking at the rubbish left behind from the fair: rotten apples, maggoty cabbages, anything that might possibly be eaten. Reuben felt the chill in the air suddenly biting at his bones. He looked at Flyte.

Flyte, tight-lipped and nervous, was quickly packing up the remaining bottles, stuffing them haphazardly into the boxes.

'Hurry up!' Flyte barked. 'Get it away. Move. Did you hear me? I won't mention that broken bottle, eh?'

Reuben went cold all over. How had Flyte seen that broken bottle? The thing had just slipped from his nervous, cold fingers and split in two on the cobbles. Surely Flyte hadn't seen it? How did he *know*? It must be true then, that he never took his eyes off him . . . Thank the Lord he hadn't tried to escape today. His skin tingled with relief – Flyte would definitely have seen him go.

Flyte kept glancing back over his shoulder, fiddling with his hat and hissing through his teeth. He pulled harshly at Nellie, fitting her roughly back into the shafts and buckling up the harness swiftly with practised fingers. He unfurled the covers to hide the writing on the sides of the wagon and jumped nimbly up onto the seat.

'Go!'

Reuben wasn't sure which frightened him the most – Flyte being friendly, or Flyte being nervous.

Flyte was as still as a statue beside him as Nellie trotted out of the village and they rumbled down the lane. Reuben searched along the road for the dog. Where had she been all this while? Maybe someone had caught her? Maybe she hadn't followed them into the village? *Please don't desert me, Shadow,* he begged.

They passed an elderly couple walking back from the village and Flyte called out a cheery 'good evening' to them, lifting off his hat politely, but Reuben noticed Flyte's hand was trembling and that he gripped the rim of his hat so tightly his knuckles showed white.

Reuben leaned against the far side of the swaying wagon, shut his eyes, and tried to disappear into the fabric, into its wooden sides and old leathery smell. He shut his eyes so there would be no chance of seeing that thin woman with her sick son, George. Or Flyte, or Baggs or anything.

He would think about his grandmother . . .

10
A Barn in Willsbridge

It was Farmer Sneddon, whose son Rufus had been paralysed, who led the campaign to bring Sarah Mearbeck to justice – with the enthusiastic help of Meg Silver.

The nearest court was in Exeter. Exeter, Mister Sneddon pronounced, was too far. 'Mistress Mearbeck'll have to sit in a prison cell until the end of April, waiting for the assize court judge to arrive,' he said. 'She'll be dead by then. I'm not having her cheat us of a good hanging!'

So they took her to Willsbridge, the nearest small town where there were several gentlemen who would all happily agree – while they took a glass of port wine with Squire Sneddon – that there was more than enough evidence to hang her as a witch.

Meg Silver gave a clear account of the events. She read out a long, long list of complaints against Reuben's grandmother. Even the twisted old roots which hung above the fire drying, ready to make into potions and poultices – those, claimed Meg Silver, were animals which came alive at night and did Sarah Mearbeck's bidding. She had seen them. So had her husband. So had her son.

It wasn't only Meg Silver. John Turnbull and Annie Purseglove, Doctor Proctor and Mister Gowdie, the apothecary, all signed papers to certify that Sarah Mearbeck had practised witchcraft against them, causing them to have seizures, cramps, blinding head pains and convulsions.

For a whole week, Reuben sat on the hard, cold earth outside the barn where they were keeping his grandmother, leaning his bony back against the tall wooden doors, shoulders hunched against the cold. He didn't think anything much. If a mind can be empty, his was pretty close.

'Reuben?'

'Yes, Granny.' He turned and whispered through the gap between the doors. 'Yes, I'm here.' He rested his cheek against the cold wood. He could hear the shuffle of her clothes, like bird's feathers, as she moved just inches away on the other side of the door. Her breathing was heavy and made a hoarse, grating noise, as if it was sticking in her throat.

'Reuben, dear boy,' she croaked. 'When I heard that your mother and father died, I thought I'd soon follow, dying from grief, if not from the fever.' She paused to cough, then went on. 'But I didn't. I had to be strong to look after you. You and I must be made of mighty powerful stuff.'

'Yes,' agreed Reuben, though he didn't feel it at this

moment. He stared down at his hands, white and thin like skeleton hands, and his knees so sharp they had burst through his breeches. When had he last eaten? He was fading away . . . I shall disappear when Granny does, he thought, and have done with it all.

'My life on this earth might be finished, Reuben, but yours isn't and I forbid you to give up because of me, hear me?' There was a long pause while she gathered her strength to go on. 'You must go to Stonebridge – I've cousins . . . I was born there. It's a distance, but our kin will help you. The likes of Meg Silver, they'll make it hard for you to stay . . .' She broke off, coughing and wheezing.

'Don't fret, Granny. Hush.'

'This is nothing. Nothing. I'd have died soon, anyway. I'm worn thin to snapping point. Don't want to leave you, though. You know . . . you know that you'll never be on your own. I'll be keeping you safe.'

'Hush. You're exhausting yourself,' said Reuben.

His grandmother's voice was hardly more than a whisper. 'Might as well use this bit of breath for good purpose.' And she cackled softly. 'I should've got you out of the village, before all this. Taken you to a big town, a place no one would ever notice us.'

'Yes, Granny. It doesn't matter.' He closed his eyes and sighed. It really didn't matter. Nothing mattered now.

'Reuben, Reuben!' She put fire in her voice. 'Don't you give up, boy!' She banged on the wooden door with something hard. 'Don't you sound like a dish rag to your old granny. I beg you, be strong! Change your name. Forget me. Wipe me out of your head. Go on with your life. If folks know your grandmother was hanged as a witch you'll never get work, lodgings, nothing. You must promise me, now! Strong. True. My Reuben.'

Tears began to dribble down his cheeks. 'Granny, don't say these things. Don't. There's still a chance they'll change their minds, isn't there? This can't be the end – I heard men talking in the square, saying it was years since anyone had been accused of witchcraft. They said you were innocent. There might be hope–'

'Reuben . . . There's nothing – really – nothing you can do . . .'

'Nothing? Nothing?' Reuben had heard the slightest hesitation in her voice. 'I'll do anything!'

He pressed his face against the door until the knots and grooves of the wood pressed into his flesh. 'Granny! Please tell me. It'll make it easier for me if I could just do something! Anything.'

The only sound through the door was his grandmother's laboured breathing: had she collapsed? Fallen asleep?

'There's one thing.' Her voice came at last. 'It's wrong of me to ask – it's not fair of me to – but I'm an old woman, and God forgive me, I'm weak . . .' She broke off and Reuben imagined her trying to get strength to speak. 'Truth is, I'm scared, Reuben. There is one last favour I ask of you . . .'

11
Flyte's Hideout

The wagon's wheel hit a rut in the road, jolting Reuben awake. He blinked, caught between the real world and his memory, unsure of himself.

Night was drawing in: dark, damp and cold. Where was Baggs? And where was Shadow? He looked backwards into the darkness, hoping to catch a glimpse of pale shaggy fur somewhere behind them.

'There he is,' grunted Flyte, and Reuben's hopes suddenly soared, thinking it was the dog, but Flyte meant the light which had appeared ahead, swinging from side to side. The yellow dot seemed to float out from beneath the blackness of the tree, unattached to anything, but as the wagon slowed down, Reuben saw it was a lantern swinging from Baggs's hand. In his other hand, two dead chickens hung limply.

'Good work, Baggs,' Flyte muttered.

Baggs climbed up into his seat between them and nodded in acknowledgement. 'Ta.'

He slipped his hand into the space between his and Reuben's thighs and pinched the boy's flesh viciously.

'Enjoy the show, Milksop?'

'Yes,' said Reuben, determined not to show he was

hurt. 'It was excellent,' he added. 'You should have been there. Doctor Flyte's medicine is very strong. He cured a man right there and then. A man with stones.'

Baggs roared with laughter. 'You stupid little fart!' he said. 'Are you such a dolt? Such a fool?'

Reuben shrank, waiting for another pinch or blow.

'It was me, you cretin!' In a deep, different voice, he said: '*Stones are so painful! They burn up me insides and twist me guts!* It was *me* with the eye patch and the stones, clot! I was so good, I hoodwinked you, didn't I?'

'Would've deceived your own mother,' said Flyte, laughing. 'If you had one!'

It shocked Reuben as much as a punch in the stomach would have. 'No! It couldn't have been! He had no spots!'

That brought a punch on the leg. 'Spots be damned!' roared Baggs. 'I covered me spots with lotion. Didn't you think me very pale?'

Reuben nodded.

'I go round the crowd before Doctor Flyte starts up,' Baggs went on. 'Find out folk's ailments. Me and the doctor have got a code, see: a little twitch, a wave or wink, and Doctor knows what's up with them. It works a treat.'

'But that, that means . . .' He didn't dare say it out loud. The doctor wasn't looking for signs of illness when he held the people's hands. And the medicine didn't work!

It was lies!

Doctor Flyte was a *quack*!

Poor little George: he wasn't going to get better. His mother was three precious pennies worse off and her son was just as sick as before. And *I* sold it to her! he thought. I lied and cheated them. He felt sweat suddenly breaking out and his heart thumped wildly.

No wonder Flyte had been nervous at the end!

No wonder they'd had to flee so fast – in case anyone who'd bought the formula had realised how useless it was. Oh, Granny, forgive me!

'If you weren't as ugly as a pig's backside, you could have gone on the stage, Baggs,' chuckled Flyte.

They travelled for hours through the dark, the lanterns on the wagon the only illumination in the country lanes and paths.

With nothing to look at, Reuben listened: to the mud squelching beneath the wheels, the rush of water as they crossed over bridges, the whine of the wind through a forest of beech trees. Occasionally they passed cottages and farms where windows showed cracks of yellow light. Reuben imagined the happy families inside, huddled round the fire, talking together. Safe. He could almost feel the warmth locked in behind the shutters.

At last, they seemed to be getting somewhere. The wagon slowed down as it manoeuvred down a steep hill;

the ground was bumpy and rocky. Tall trees sighed and moaned around them. Nellie's hooves clacked against the flints on the path.

Taking the lantern, Baggs jumped down from the wagon and lit the way ahead. A small stone cottage, nothing more than a hovel with a broken thatch and a door hanging on sagging hinges, came into view.

'Home sweet home,' said Flyte.

Baggs undid the traces and released Nellie. 'I'll do the horse,' he said. He handed the second lantern to Flyte before disappearing behind the building.

Flyte beckoned to Reuben to get down, then, unlocking the wooden door, he led him into the one-roomed cottage, holding the lantern high. There was a hardened mud floor covered with mouldy reeds, which the mice had been nibbling. The smell from the old reeds was pungent and damp, clogging his nostrils. There were piles of clothes and scraps of wood in the corners. Two stools, a battered, scarred table beneath the window, and some mattresses, were the only bits of furniture. The hearth was a mountain of cold ashes and white bones.

'As it should be,' Flyte said, peering round. 'Get started on the food, boy. Two hens. Fire needs lighting. Wood outside, and remember–' he lay his hand on Reuben's shoulder '– me and Baggs know the lie of this land. Don't think about running. We'd have you in no time at all – and Reuben?' he added.

'Yes?'

'This time I won't treat insolent behaviour so leniently. I've been wanting to try my hand at tooth-pulling,' he added with a leer. 'I'm not so able at it yet. Customers have said I'm too rough, too slow. It's practice I need. D'you see?'

'I do see,' said Reuben, nodding. 'Yes, Doctor Flyte.' And he scuttled outside.

Immediately he was plunged into darkness. He made his way round behind the cottage by feeling along the rough stone walls, tripping and stumbling through shrubs and bramble, and over boulders. Round the corner of the building, he saw at last the glow of Baggs's lantern.

'He sent me looking for wood,' Reuben said.

'Did he indeed?' said Baggs, grinning spitefully at him.

Reuben nodded.

'Well, get looking, then,' said Baggs, turning smartly. He strode off, holding the lantern in front of him, plunging Reuben into the pitch black of the night again. Reuben heard him laughing as he disappeared.

'Thanks, Baggs,' he muttered.

He kept very still, feeling the thickness of the night surround him. He closed his eyes and it was the same. Darkness. Nothing. I could run, he thought, they say they could get me, but they never would; I'm younger, faster . . . But I daren't. Ground's treacherous with those sharp, flinty stones in the grass, and all those trees. A man in Birtwell Priory had run straight at a tree in the dark and killed himself. Where would I go, anyway? Nobody wants me. Nobody cares about me at all. Flyte'd catch me and Flyte, oh, he'd do something so bad . . . No, I'll wait. Chance will come.

He rubbed at his eyes and realised he was beginning to make out a little of what was around him. He could see some pale tree trunks, the cottage wall and roof. He could hear Baggs and Flyte's laughter coming from inside the building.

Wood. Wood, he reminded himself, find some wood for the fire. I'm hungry. Starving. It's hours and hours since we've had a bite. My head aches from that wretched wagon. Must get wood before Flyte gets mad!

Something moved in the dark, a blacker shape against the black night.

Reuben went rigid with fear.

'Who's there?'

Another movement – something there in the grass.

'Who is it? Come out! Baggs?'

No, it was small, an animal. A fox? Cat? He heard a soft whimper. Was it a whimper? It was!

Shadow.

'Shadow!' he called softly. 'Good dog.' The dog came over to him and let Reuben pat her head. Her tail swished back and forth. 'Good dog. I'm so pleased to see you. I'll bring you food,' he promised, feeling the dog was waiting for something. 'I'll get you some chicken bones. That'll be good, won't it? And bread?' He tried to put his arms round the dog, but she backed away nervously. 'All right, you don't quite trust me, do you? That's all right. I understand.'

The dog whined and slunk back into the dark. He heard her whining from a few feet away, but he couldn't see her.

'I can't come,' he hissed in her direction. 'It's too dangerous; they'll get me.'

He felt her sitting and waiting, watching him in the darkness.

'Sorry, Shadow,' he whispered. 'I can't come now.'

He set about searching for firewood happily. Shadow was there. He was not alone.

Flyte and Baggs had almost finished plucking the chickens when Reuben stumbled back in, his arms full of fallen branches and twigs.

Baggs glared at him and spat on the floor. 'Took your time, didn't you?'

Flyte was drinking rum from a small, thick glass. He blew a long stream of smoke from his pipe. 'Plenty of time. All the time in the world.'

Reuben tumbled the wood into the fireplace. Some of it was a little green, he noticed now, but it would probably burn well enough.

Baggs went out to unload the wagon, bringing in boxes and bags, bundles of clothes and books, bottles and jars. When he saw the fire, he stopped suddenly.

'What wood's that?' he demanded, pointing at the flames beginning to flicker hotly up the chimney.

'From behind the cottage,' said Reuben.

'But what *wood* is it?'

'I don't know. Apple tree and hazel and that looks like elder wood–'

'Elder! Elder!' Baggs snatched his hat off and threw it to the floor. 'Flyte! He's burning elder in your cottage.'

Flyte ignored him.

'What's wrong?' asked Reuben, though he guessed quickly enough, when he saw Baggs snatching up the smouldering elder sticks and tossing them outside.

'What are you trying to do to us, puddinghead?' Baggs knelt on the floor, poking anxiously at the fire, checking he'd removed all the elder wood. '*You* should know about that wood!'

Reuben shook his head and shrugged.

'It's always scared me, has that stuff,' said Baggs, looking up at Flyte for support. 'I remember, when I was small, at that old Mother Margaret's – she looked after lots of us children, babies too – and she had this baby, only it wouldn't stop crying.' Baggs gazed into the fire as if he could see and hear the baby right there in the grate. 'The rockers on its cradle had got broke and she'd sent out a lad to mend it and he'd mended it with elder wood – mended the rockers . . . And now the cradle rocked and rocked, wild as a mad thing, even when no one was around. It rocked so wildly the baby got flung out and crashed its skull on the stone floor. That stopped it crying. It was dead. I remember that.' He glared at Reuben. 'See, you should never use elder, it's a bad wood . . . I 'spect your old grandmother used it?'

Reuben shook his head. 'She wasn't a–'

'Witches disguise themselves in elder trees,' went on Baggs, ignoring him. 'I saw it myself, how an elder twig can bleed. We cut a twig from the elder and it bled real blood. Then we saw this old woman who we'd always thought were a witch and she was bleeding from her arm too. It proved she were a witch, see?'

Reuben didn't say anything. It was the stuff all the village children talked; superstitious stories.

'Don't never bring elder into the house, again, Reuben,' warned Baggs, 'or it'll be the worse for you.'

Flyte took his pipe from his mouth and with his eyes shut, sang:

'Hawthorn bloom and elder flowers
Fill the house with evil powers!'

He snorted, a laugh or a contemptuous 'Blah!'

'There. See,' said Baggs, matter of factly. 'Doctor knows. Only way you might bring it inside – is you cut a piece off that the sun ain't shone on, cut it between two knots and wear the twig around the neck. That stops you getting fits, that does. I hope you ain't brought no evil into the cottage,' he went on, feeling half-heartedly for something around his neck which wasn't there. 'Bad luck, that is, such bad luck.'

He went back to emptying the wagon, muttering to himself and shaking his head.

'That lad'd talk the hind leg off a bloody donkey if you let him,' said Flyte. 'Only thing is, I don't!'

At last the fire was burning well and the room was filled with the smell of the birds' roasting flesh.

Baggs took some rum and lit himself a pipe. 'Ah, best virginnie tobacco.' He sighed with satisfaction.

The smell of tobacco and rum, wood smoke and chicken hung heavily in the room. 'Ain't this just the life!' Baggs smiled.

Reuben closed his eyes and pictured Pleck Cottage. He remembered how cruelly it had been snatched from him when he'd returned to Birtwell Priory after his grandmother's death . . .

12
The Curse on Pleck Cottage

It was the most beautiful night that Reuben could ever remember. The moon was a giant silver coin in the sky, bathing the road in whiteness, giving him a moon shadow. Every bare tree branch, and every blade of grass and twig and leaf, was jewelled with silvery frost, sparkling and still.

The only sound was Reuben's heavy leather boots crunching over the frozen earth and grass, clanging sharply when they kicked against stones.

He stared ahead, through his cloudy breath, to the far end of the lane as it wound away in the dark ahead of him, seeming to grow longer and longer as he walked down it. He was going home. Home.

It was six miles from Willsbridge to Birtwell Priory and Pleck Cottage and tonight the journey was so long and so slow he began to doubt he'd ever reach it. He was weary and as cold and unfeeling as a stone. He had been gone for only seven days, but it felt like a year. His grandmother was dead, hanged as a witch and he was never going to see her again.

What else could he do but go home to Pleck Cottage?

It was daybreak when Reuben arrived. A cold, clear

morning with a white sort of sunshine. He stood beside the dead tree stump and stared at his cottage.

It's shrunk, he thought, or is it just that the barn at Willsbridge was so tall with such high wooden doors? And the houses and streets there were bigger too?

Despite the sunshine, the cottage looked cold, but that was natural if the fire had gone out. But no – there was smoke coming from the chimney. The whole place, now he looked around, was different; as if little things, tiny things, had been shifted about. What was it?

The cottage door opened as Reuben walked towards it. Oliver Silver, Meg's large son, appeared on the threshold.

Reuben was so surprised, his legs buckled.

What?

I'm half-witted! The fairies have knotted my brains in Willsbridge, he thought. Isn't that Ollie Silver there? On our doorstep?

'Reuben! Lord, Reuben! I never thought . . .' Oliver began, stepping forward, back, forward again. 'It's over then? She's . . . dead?' He almost held out his hand to Reuben, then didn't. 'I am sorry, honest I am,' he said. 'You poor lad. Was it terrible?'

'She's gone. I'll never see her again,' said Reuben, staring up at him without really seeing him. 'She was everything. I've got nothing.'

'I know. I'm sorry. Sorry about this, the cottage, about

my mother – Reuben, you've changed. You look – well, older, smaller, thinner,' said Oliver, raking his fingers through his hair. 'Are you well?'

Reuben didn't speak. It was true. He was different. He'd never be the same again.

'Now, see here, Reuben, this is awkward . . . See, we didn't expect you back,' said Oliver, stepping out at last and pulling the door shut behind him. 'We thought you'd stay away.'

'You didn't expect me back?' said Reuben. 'To my home?'

'Well . . .' Oliver suddenly darted a look over Reuben's shoulder. Reuben turned too. Meg Silver was racing towards them, puffing and blowing with excitement, her skirt bundled up in her hands.

Meg Silver. His stomach heaved, his throat tightened, he felt his cheeks blazing red. He quickly closed his eyes, blocking her out, never wanting to see her again. He felt hot, fiery vomit at the back of his throat and swallowed it back.

More bad things were going to happen, Reuben could sense it. He cracked a lopsided smile at Oliver. 'What is it?' he managed to ask. 'What's going on?'

White flashes of light leaped in at the edges of his vision. He tried to blink them away.

'You see . . .' Oliver began, not unkindly, then stopped as his mother reached them.

'Reuben!' She pulled her satin purse with the toad's leg in it from its hiding place and squeezed her fingers round it. 'Now, Reuben. We didn't think you'd be back,' she said. 'Well, we didn't. And you can't keep living here, can you? Not a wee lad like you, all on your own? Who'd look after you? What would you do, eh? That's what we wondered.'

Reuben stared at her, trying to make some sense of her words. All he could think was that she was the ugliest woman he'd ever seen and the way her mouth pulled down at the corners made her look meaner than a mad goat. And that he wanted to leap at her and gouge her eyes out with his bare fingers. He pushed his hands deep into his pockets, already feeling her flesh and rubbery eyeballs exploding against his skin.

'So, Oliver here is having it,' went on Meg. 'He needs a place. His Sally won't marry him till there's a house for them to go to and you know there's nothing empty in the village. When he's in a cottage he can get married, can't he?' She nodded, agreeing with herself. 'He *needs* Pleck Cottage, Reuben.'

What did she mean? It wasn't possible. Reuben looked at her blankly.

'What about the bees? The garden?' he heard himself ask.

In his pockets his fingers squirmed and dug at her.

'That'll be grand,' said Oliver. 'We're going to keep pigs and some chickens. Don't you worry.'

Reuben knew he was beaten. I don't want to stay here anyway! he wanted to shout at them. This is Granny's place. Our place.

'What about Granny's things? You didn't touch her things?'

'Most got burned, see, as safest thing to do,' said Oliver, smiling hopefully. 'You know, folk were worried about stuff being cursed and that . . . I put one or two things aside for you, though; things I thought you'd want if you did come back . . .'

He stood aside and opened the door.

Reuben had been ready to charge in and grab everything, but when he looked in at the room he'd known all his life as home, home wasn't there.

Gone were his grandmother's bed and the patchwork quilt she'd made for her wedding day. Gone were the pewter candlesticks and the three-legged stool beside the fire. Gone were her books and her shawl and her green apron that hung beside the hearth.

'I've put a few things here, you see,' said Oliver. 'Some clothes and your Bible, in case you did come back. Your granny's pestle and mortar.'

Reuben held out his arms for the bundle. Mine! he wanted to shout. Don't touch them, they're mine.

Oliver pushed them gently into his arms. 'See, I'm

going to make it snug and get Sally for a wife. That'll be fine, won't it? And you'd want a family in here, wouldn't you?'

Reuben didn't, couldn't say anything.

'There, good boy. You'll find somewhere else. Jess Greeve said you could bed down with them for a while, till you're fixed. Churchwarden's going to find you a place of work, what d'you think of that? Maybe up at Holme Farm?'

Reuben nodded, hardly breathing. Never. Never! he thought. I won't stay here. I shouldn't have come back, but I'm glad I did, now I know there's nothing here for me.

'But there is just one thing troubling Oliver,' Meg said, squinting at him, lowering her voice. 'We want to know – I know you'll tell me the truth, won't you lad – are there things in the cottage? Or out in the yard? You know, things old Sarah used for her curses? Reuben, are you listening? Might there be dead cats hidden in the walls? Dead babies in the yard?'

Reuben stared: was the women crazed? Her eyes were bulging like a frog's, as if she were about to burst. He pictured himself popping her fat cheeks with a pointed stick. Maybe she *was* mad. Maybe he could make her mad.

'Yes,' he said.

'Oh!' Meg drew back, clutching her purse. 'There! I

told you, Oliver! We'll have to tread careful! The ground's frozen solid too and we can't go digging yet.'

'Where?' asked Oliver. Fear made his big, moon-like face whiter and rounder than ever.

'I'm not certain. She never told me. It was a secret.'

'Oh, Oliver! We'll have to pull it all to bits to find them!' groaned Meg.

'A horse's skull,' said Reuben slowly, as if remembering. 'I seem to recall . . . under the floor. Perhaps the scullery? It was secret, she didn't tell me everything.' He took a step towards the door. 'I'll be on my way, then,' he added, squeezing the bundle in his arms. 'I'll walk on up to Holme Farm and see the Greeves about that place.'

'Oh, yes, do go!' It was a sigh of relief from Meg. 'Start afresh, eh?'

Reuben nodded and backed out.

'Good luck to you, Reuben!' called Oliver. Then to his mother in a small voice: 'Oh, Mother, what shall we do?' He moved his fingers up and down the doorframe nervously, as if feeling for the hidden spells and charms that Sarah Mearbeck might have left behind. 'What shall we do?'

Reuben turned and walked away through the village on crumbling legs, lights like daggers, sharp and blinding, at the edges of his eyes.

Grand-mo-ther, Grand-mo-ther, Grand-mo-ther, each

step a syllable. He didn't know what to say, what to think. In his mind there was only her. Images of her moving around the cottage, stroking his head, stirring food in the big black pot, making medicines.

Grand-mo-ther . . .

He walked to the edge of the village where the Gratton's barn stood open and last year's hay was stacked. Sinking down in it, he covered his head in his arms and wept.

He must have slept.

He was woken by someone kicking him gently. 'Oy, is that you, little Reuben? You can't sleep here.'

He rubbed his eyes and looked up at the surprised face of Ellen Gratton.

'Ellen!' His smile faded as soon as it came, recalling what had happened. 'Ellen, they've thrown me out of my home! Meg Silver and her son.'

' 'Course they have. They would, wouldn't they? Everyone's scared of you, Ruby. Was she really a witch, your granny? She never put a spell on me. Mistress Trimble says she put a curse on her spinning wheel and made it go slow. Did she?'

Reuben shook his head. 'It's lies. Meg Silver's lies.'

'Well, there's nothing you can do, Reuben, and you can't stay here, neither. If Dad found you, he'd think you were putting a spell on the hay, making it go bad or something. They're suspicious of their own shadows, they are.'

'Aren't you scared, then?' asked Reuben.

'No. You wouldn't hurt me, would you? You gave me a whole basket of cherries last year and I kissed you once.'

Reuben nodded. 'I don't know what to do . . . I haven't got anyone – anything.'

'And I bet you're hungry?'

He nodded.

'Well, I'll bring you some food, then you must go. Honest, you can't stay . . . Is she really dead? Was it bad? They say when a witch is hanged, her familiars leap out of her mouth and run off to seek a new mistress. Did you see them? Did the Devil show himself? Did she scream when she died? Did she–'

'Ellen, she was just my granny. Sarah Mearbeck wasn't a witch.'

'Well, everyone says she was.' She made a face. 'Ah, well, I'll go find you a bit of cheese.'

After he'd eaten, Reuben felt better. Ellen sat on the wall beside him, swinging her legs. 'Where you going then?'

'Not sure. Well, south, towards Trowbridge,' he lied. He didn't want anyone coming after him.

'I won't tell a soul I've seen you,' she said. 'If you'll give me a kiss.'

He pecked her cheek. ' 'Bye, Ellen.'

' 'Bye, Ruby.'

The kiss so confused him that he left his bundle – his cloak, his grandmother's Bible and papers – left it all behind as he set off walking, thinking only of Ellen's soft cheek and how different it had felt compared to putting his lips against his grandmother's cheek, which had been like kissing a pear that had over-wintered in a warm barn, dry and wrinkled.

In a trance, Reuben took the road north towards Longford, and that was how he came to be picked up by Doctor Flyte and Baggs.

13
The Fishing Accident

When Reuben woke late the next morning, Flyte's cottage was deserted.

It was an even more dismal place in the harsh light of the day.

Cracks showed in the grubby wattle and daub walls; cobwebs thick with dust hung like tattered curtains from the rafters. Rat droppings littered the floor. The shutters at the window were broken, held up with rope and patched with fragments of board. There was a wet patch where rainwater had come through the roof.

Reuben sat up, but when he tried to stand, he found he couldn't: his ankles were tied together. There must have been a rope around his wrists too, which had gone now, because they were red and showed indentations from where the knots had pressed into his flesh. He had slept so deeply they had been able to truss him up like a chicken.

He unfastened the rope and went to the open doorway, squinting against the sunshine. Nellie, hobbled on a long rope, was grazing on fresh grass. The air was charged with birdsong. It was warm. Spring was coming – Granny's favourite time, he thought.

The cottage was on a slope, surrounded by a rich forest of hazel, birch and ancient gnarled oaks. Reuben stood very still. He thought he heard the trees crackle softly and murmur, as if they were slowly unfurling. The feeling of hope and newness all around him sent a delightful shiver up his spine.

They can't watch me every minute here, he thought, inhaling deeply, feeling taller. Can't tie me up during the day like old Nellie. I'll run amongst the trees and bushes and away! Then he remembered how Flyte had seen him drop that bottle of formula at the fair, how he'd heard him on that first night, when he tried to creep off . . .

Escape was not going to be easy.

Reuben peered through the trees and splintered sunlight. About thirty feet away Flyte and Baggs were sitting in the dappled shade, beside a river. The sound of running water had been in the background, he realised now, without him being aware of it.

'Reuben! Come!' called Flyte. He had an uncanny way of seeing Reuben wherever he was.

Reuben went to them along a tiny, overgrown path leading from cottage door to riverbank; his feet crushed leaves and plants and a rich scent rose up as he passed. He inhaled deeply, loving the scent, the closest idea of 'green' that he knew.

Flyte was sitting on the ground, leaning back against a

large, smooth rock, chewing on the stem of his pipe. His head looked small and insubstantial without its customary hat.

'Baggs is after catching us trout for dinner,' Flyte said to Reuben in a jovial voice.

'Or toad, more like,' said Baggs. 'It's swarming with them dirty hoppers.'

'I can hear them,' said Reuben, glancing at the network of muddy ditches of water beside the river where he knew they'd be. The river was the width of two good horses, nose to tail. The water was fast flowing and deep, good for trout, but not for toads.

'What d'you think of my abode?' asked Flyte, nodding back towards the tiny cottage.

'It's . . . very well hidden,' said Reuben, carefully.

Flyte chuckled. 'True.'

'Listen to those old toads!' said Baggs, who was tying bait to the end of his fishing line. 'I can't abide that racket! What do they do it for?'

'That's the males, calling for a female,' said Reuben. 'I used to sit and watch them in the stream at home. It's interesting. I think the females like the noise and–'

He broke off as Baggs doubled up with silent laughter.

'What? Singing, like little birdies?' he roared. 'I never knew toads could *sing*!'

Doctor Flyte spat out a shred of tobacco. 'Trouts shall sing the chorus, eh, Reuben?'

Reuben opened his mouth, ready to retaliate, but thought better, swallowed hard and looked away.

'Your arse'll sing a song of the leather strap, Baggs, if we don't get some fish in soon,' said Flyte. 'Get that hook in the water, lad!'

Baggs tossed the baited hook far out into the river.

'Are we staying here for a long time, Doctor Flyte?' Reuben asked, tentatively.

'Maybe.'

'Doctor Flyte's got plans,' said Baggs. 'Not that he'd tell you, Squit-face!' He lifted the copper hook clear of the water and then dropped it in again. 'Shame we've only got worms for bait,' he added. 'Bit of lung's good, or liver. Fish like liver best of all.'

'Is that what they tell you, Baggs?' scoffed Flyte. 'Well, I never.'

Baggs went red.

'Where shall we be going next?' asked Reuben.

'There's a fair at – a place nearby. I'll require your particular assistance, Reuben.'

'Me?'

'Yes, you, Scum-face,' said Baggs. 'You can be put to some use, can't you? Earn your keep. Pay Doctor Flyte back for his kindness in feeding you and buying you cloaks and everything.'

'I didn't ask for the cloak, I–' said Reuben.

Doctor Flyte took his pipe from his mouth, his lips

narrowed, his brows came down and everything about him seemed to harden and grow cold. For a second Reuben thought the sun had gone in.

Flyte didn't stare straight into Reuben's eyes; his look was slightly unfocused, as if there was something more interesting going on behind Reuben's back. Reuben knew he was in trouble. He wished his thoughtless words could jump back in his mouth.

'I mean, I mean . . .' he stuttered.

'How's that?' Flyte lay down his pipe very slowly and sat forward. 'You didn't ask for the cloak?' Now he was kneeling. 'You'd rather be lying in the ditch? Cold?' He was on his feet. 'Starving?' He was striding towards him. 'Is that what you mean?' He was inches away.

Reuben found himself staring at Flyte's crooked nose, the bristles poking out from the skin on his dirty cheek, a crumb caught beside his mouth.

'I meant, only – I only meant that I didn't want to be–'

But Flyte was on him, both big hands clutching at his throat, forcing his breath out, his head back. 'Yes?' he snarled. 'Yes?'

'Kill him, Doctor!' Baggs jumped to his feet.

But Baggs had forgotten his fishing rod.

The line and hook whipped out of the water, the metal hook spun through the air – a flash of copper, like a shiny insect, as it flew.

'Ow!' Baggs clutched his cheek. The hook had speared

his face. 'Ow!' Baggs snatched at it, yelping in pain. 'Ow! Ow!'

His whole body jerked and he toppled forward, his boot came down on the line, pulling it tight and the hook ripped deeper into his flesh.

'My face! My face!' Baggs yelped, clutching at his face, then at the line. Blood began to ooze out around his fingers. 'Help!'

'You great clumsy lummock!' roared Flyte, kicking Baggs's foot off the line to loosen it. 'Hold your gulsh, you sound like a cat on fire!'

'Sorry. Sorry.' Baggs ran his fingers nervously round the embedded hook. 'It's gone right in. It hurts,' he whimpered. 'It bloody hurts.'

Reuben's heart was racing. His throat hurt from Flyte's tight fist; he couldn't swallow and could hardly breathe. He scrambled a distance away, watching.

The air seemed full of the sound of the croaking, singing toads.

'Don't move, boy!' Flyte warned Reuben. 'You, Baggs, keep still. Let's look at it.'

Flyte knelt beside Baggs, pushing his head round till the sunlight fell directly on the injured cheek. 'Ah, it's nothing much. Lucky it missed your eye. Won't spoil your looks. I'll cut it.' He took his knife from his belt.

'Oh, don't. It'll hurt. Don't touch me!'

'Just cutting the line, Baggsy.' He sliced the horse hair

fishing line close to the hook. 'There. Not strung up like a fish.'

'Thank you, Doctor.' Baggs got slowly to his feet. Holding his big hand over the hook, and backing away, he sobbed: 'It hurts. I need a surgeon.' There was a trickle of blood escaping from the wound.

'No.' Flyte shook his head. 'I'm a doctor, trust me.'

'The barb's right in,' Reuben said quietly, 'and a surg–'

'Shut it!' roared Baggs, kicking at him. 'Don't want your pennyworth!'

Reuben dodged his heavy boot. 'It's just, I know a good poultice, one my granny used for this sort–'

'No witchcraft! No magic on me!' said Baggs, flaring at Reuben. 'Leave me alone.'

He got up and staggered up the hill, careening wildly through the bushes. He slammed the cottage door behind him with such a crash, birds rose from the surrounding trees.

Reuben sat very still. He watched a fly come down to feast on a drop of Baggs's blood. He heard a fish flick the surface of the water.

Doctor Flyte sighed and leaned back against the lichen-covered rock. He squinted at the water as if he could see down to its deepest depths, and chewed a stem of grass as if nothing had happened.

Reuben waited.

Flyte had not put his knife back into its sheath. Now

he began to slowly rub the flat of the blade over the smooth stone beside him. He splashed the stone with water from the bucket, keeping it moist. The grating, grainy sound of the blade on the stone set Reuben's teeth on edge. He waited.

'Poultices?' said Flyte, at last, examining the fine edge on his blade. 'What else? Curses? How to talk to the spirits? Call up her familiars?' He swivelled round and grinned at Reuben, twisting the blade in front of his face, watching it glint in the sun. 'Come on, boy. Time to talk. Time to tell me. How *did* she make Old John drop dead like that?'

'Doctor Flyte, Doctor Flyte, no!' Reuben begged him. 'She didn't. I never–'

'But I know, Reuben. Why d'you think we followed you out of town and picked you up? Why would we bother with a scurvy little beetle like you, otherwise?'

'I don't know. I don't know why you did,' said Reuben.

'Let's say, you've got something I need.'

'I haven't got anything!'

'But you have. You deny it, but you have.'

Reuben scratched at the moss beneath his fingers and waited.

'In your nonce. Things old Mistress Mearbeck told you. I knew her when she was younger, you know. Yes, you're surprised. 'Tis a long time ago now. She could do magic then, too; curse and cure.' He took out his pipe from his jacket pocket and stuck it between his teeth. He went on staring at the water.

It seemed to Reuben that in the quiet the toads started calling again, a weary croaking and coughing sound.

Flyte took the pipe from his mouth. 'I want you to put a curse on a man,' he went on at last. 'A bad man it is, Reuben, so your conscience won't be troubled. Now I've got you, I can punish him. That's fair. What he deserves. He lives in this place we're going to.' He tapped his pipe on the rock. 'No tobacco,' he grumbled, and made ready to go back up to the cottage.

'I can't do curses,' said Reuben. 'Nobody can.'

Flyte went very still, a cat ready to pounce.

'Don't tell me that. You can. I'll make you do it, Reuben. I will skin your weedy little body if you don't, starting with your fingers, Reuben, so it won't hurt enough to stop your breath; peeling back the soft pink, slowly, slowly, just like peeling off a glove; just like we skin the rabbits, I'll turn you inside out and then dangle you from a tree so the ravens come and peck at your innards . . .'

Reuben knew Flyte was capable of carrying out his threat, but mixed with his fear, was contempt. You fool, you fool, Reuben wanted to say. If my granny had been able to curse people, we'd have been rich. She'd have done for that old fox, Meg Silver, most surely. You're a fool and ignoramus you are, Flyte!

'No fish for supper!' Flyte suddenly said. 'God's teeth! The boy's stupid. Not like you, eh, Reuben?' He got up and picked up the abandoned fishing rod. 'Come on. Should have had Baggs drowned before he grew so bloomin' big, eh?'

Flyte followed Reuben up the path, jabbing him in the back every few steps with the end of the rod, reminding him he was there.

Reuben gently pushed open the cottage door, nervously.

'Don't touch me!' Baggs cried, holding out an arm to keep them back. 'Get away from me.'

He was lying on his mattress on the floor. Blood had dried in brown rivulets down his cheek. His cheek and eye were beginning to swell.

'Don't!'

'Shut your pie-trap. The hook's got to come out.' Flyte set his pipe down on the table beside his hat, slicked back his hair and rubbed his hands together. 'Copper hook's too 'spensive to leave in. Now . . .'

'How?' Reuben whispered.

Reuben's insides rose up and filled his throat. His knees sagged.

'I'll do it.' Flyte grinned. 'Doctor will see to his patient, won't he, Baggs?'

'What?'

'Nothing, nothing. Should I give him some rum?' Reuben added. 'For the pain?'

Flyte nodded. Reuben poured out a large mug of rum and passed it to Flyte.

Flyte held it to Baggs's lips: 'Here, drink it!'

'I don't want it!' Baggs spluttered and choked. 'Stop! Stop! D'you want to kill me?'

'Of course we do! Now, do as I say!' Flyte knelt beside him. 'Hold him down, Reuben.'

Gingerly, Reuben moved to Baggs's other side and took his arm.

'No, no! Sit on him! Tight!' yelled Flyte. 'Go on!'

Avoiding meeting Baggs's eyes, Reuben straddled his chest, pressing his knees down onto his arms, so Baggs was pinioned to the floor. Reuben wasn't much of a weight, but Baggs lay very still, except for his eyes which rolled round crazily like marbles.

'Granny poured rum onto the wound,' said Reuben, eyeing the injury. 'Or ale or brandy, even.' He saw that the hook had disappeared beneath the flesh, only a strand of fishing line showed and the merest hint of metal. 'She said alcohol helped mend cuts and sores and–'

'Don't!' Baggs turned imploringly to Doctor Flyte. 'Nothing *she* said! Nothing to do with *her*! No witchcraft!'

'I was only–' Reuben began.

'No!'

Flyte's expression was ghastly. As he held the knife poised above Baggs, his face cracked with a wide, malicious smile. 'Still as a mouse, Baggs, or it might be your eye that pops out, and not the hook, then you'll need that eye patch for real.'

'Go on then, quick!' gasped Baggs, bracing himself. 'Cut me. You know you want to!'

'Here I come!'

Flyte set the knife-point against the swollen skin and pushed. He applied more pressure, the blade sank deeper and he began to slice alongside the hook. The blade was sharp and the skin seemed to split and peel back with surprising ease. Blood oozed up to the surface, slowly, like water rises from a boggy ground when a footstep presses it. But then, it was as if there were a hidden power behind it, and the blood began to spurt and spout, streaming over Baggs's cheek, running down his neck and dribbling into his hair.

'I think–' Reuben ventured, but the terrible expression on Flyte's face silenced him and he bit back his suggestion.

Flyte dug deeper, cut further. The blood ran. Baggs wept.

'There, that's done it!' Flyte sat back on his heels. 'There's my hook. Just need to pull it.' He grasped at the glint of copper and yanked at it with his bloodied fingers. Baggs roared and bucked; the hook was snagged, dragging at the flesh, the barbed ends were embedded too deeply.

'Ow, ow! My face'll come off! You're killing me! Stop!'

'Hold still, you idiot! The blasted thing's stuck.' Flyte roughly jiggled the hook. 'I can't get in under it,' he said, pushing the blade-point down beside the hook. 'Can't see for the damn blood.'

Baggs cried out and kicked and screamed.

Reuben swallowed nervously, words forming in his head, expiring soundlessly on his lips. No, no, you're hurting him, making it worse. Do stop! It's wrong. Stop! He hung on grimly to Baggs, pressing him back to the floor with all his weight. Fear and sickness fought together in his stomach, so it heaved and knotted in turns, and he was sure he would vomit if Flyte didn't get it over with soon.

There was blood everywhere. Flyte had made the wound jagged and so deep, now, that Reuben thought he could glimpse the pearly sheen of bone beneath.

Flyte doesn't know anything! Reuben glanced up at him furtively and saw a maniacal grin on Flyte's face. He doesn't even care! The quack! If poison sets in, Baggs'll die. And even if it doesn't, his face will be such a mess. He remembered, suddenly, what his grandmother had once done.

'Doctor Flyte, Doctor Flyte!' Reuben yelled.

'What?' The doctor sat back, blood dripping from the knife in his hand.

'I've an idea.' Better not mention his grandmother.

'Make a little cut up there, where the tip of the hook is, then push the hook out that way. It'll go smoothly, won't it, 'cos you won't be pulling against the barbs – there's nothing to stop it?'

'Don't listen!' Baggs groaned. 'It's his fault. Aw, my, it hurts. It hurts. Don't listen to him! What does he know?'

'Interesting idea, Reuben,' Flyte whispered. 'Don't worry, Baggs,' he said more loudly. 'Shan't listen to him.'

Flyte wiped the blood clear from around the wound with his shirt-tail and quickly, before the blood started streaming again, located the hook and pushed gently on it, watching for where the skin humped up.

'There!'

Quickly he made a small incision. When he pushed the end of the hook the next time, it poked out of the new cut. He pushed it and wiggled it and the rest of it followed.

'Got it!' said Flyte. He drew the hook and line clean through the gaping hole and eyed it triumphantly. 'Got it, Baggs!'

But Baggs had fainted.

Flyte laughed. He got slowly to his feet, wiping his hands on his trousers.

'Rum, Reuben.'

Reuben slipped off Baggs's inert body and poured Flyte a fresh mug of rum. As he handed him the drink he noticed Flyte's hand was shaking. The Doctor sat at the table sipping the rum, staring down at Baggs. 'Could have been a surgeon meself,' he said. 'I've pulled teeth. Mended bones. That's the first hook.'

'It was clever of you,' Reuben said, keeping all expression from his voice and face. 'You've done a good job.'

Baggs was unconscious. His face was grey. The wound on his cheek was jagged, large and ugly, running from below his eye, down over his cheekbone. Blood dripped from it relentlessly.

'The cut needs closing up,' said Reuben.

'Don't need your advice.'

'My grandmother used a needle and thread from her sewing box.'

'Ain't no sewing box here,' laughed Flyte.

'I'll just sort of pull the bits of skin together, shall I?' said Reuben, kneeling back beside Baggs.

He grimaced: the hole was gaping and red, like another mouth. He dreaded what Baggs would say when he saw it – if he lived to see it.

Gingerly, Reuben folded the ripped skin into place, pressing the sides together and leaning gently on it, but the insides seemed bigger than they should be, and determined to spring out. The bleeding began to slow but started again as soon as he let go.

'He'll be fit enough,' said Flyte, pouring more rum. 'Leave him.'

Reuben looked around for something to make into

bandages. There was only Baggs's spare shirt. 'Sorry Baggs,' Reuben muttered quietly, and quickly he tore the grubby shirt into strips and soaked them with rum.

'We should let some blood while we're at it,' Flyte said, staring out of the window. 'The barber-surgeon drains me of eight ounces each time I see him.'

'He needs sleep,' said Reuben. His grandmother had not believed in bloodletting.

'I'll decide!' snapped Flyte. He yawned and took another gulp of his drink. 'You've too much lip, boy. Too much talk.'

Flyte was too tired and distracted to do anything, so Reuben went on with bandaging Baggs. Gritting his teeth, Reuben pressed hard on the wound with the cloth until the bleeding stopped, then he began to quickly wrap the strips of cloth tightly across Baggs's face and eye, keeping as much pressure on the cut as he dared.

Baggs's head grew into a vast, dirty turnip. Reuben sat back and admired his work. Blood seeped through the bandage, staining it dark red, but it was lessening, he was sure.

Feeling light-headed, Reuben went to the doorway and sucked in great lungfuls of fresh air.

'Don't think of it!' Flyte said without turning to look at him.

'I'm not going anywhere,' said Reuben, wearily.

Down by the river, he saw Shadow chasing something

in the undergrowth. The dog stopped and looked up towards him, as if sensing him there. Reuben hoped she'd found the bread and bones he'd hidden beneath a holly bush.

Wait for me! he begged her. *I will come soon, I promise.*

14
Flyte's Fantastic Formula

Reuben took out all the old rushes on the floor and made a bonfire of them. He swept the floor, moved the other two straw mattresses away from Baggs's corner, cleaned out the hearth and relit the fire. He pulled off the broken shutters so light came in freely at the window.

In the wagon, he found two salted pig's trotters in a sack, which he rinsed and put into a pot with potatoes and carrots and water to make a pottage. There was a bay tree growing nearby; he plucked some leaves and seasoned the soup with them.

For a few moments he was able to forget where he was and pretend he was busy in his grandmother's house, getting it ready for her return, as he often had back in Birtwell Priory. She'd taught him to cook and clean as well as read and write. And I never tried hard enough at my lessons, thought Reuben, and I will never get another chance now. He glanced through the window at Flyte, sitting on the tree stump, smoking his long clay pipe and methodically laying out the playing cards in a game. The only thing I'll learn staying here is trickery and cheating!

Flyte spent most of the day playing cards, lying on the

grass half-asleep or standing near Nellie, looking up the path, as if expecting a visitor.

Baggs slept for three hours, then at last, with a terrible groan and wail, he jerked awake, stitting up like a wooden toy, holding his hand against his bandaged cheek. He rocked back and forth.

'What you done? You nearly killed me! Water,' he moaned. 'Get me water.'

Reuben dipped the wooden ladle into the water bucket and carried it over carefully. 'Here you are, Baggs.'

He hardly dared look at him.

Baggs's face was swollen. The skin was tight and red around the bandage, as if the insides were trying to burst out. Baggs winced as he sipped the water. 'Flyte's cut my damn face off.'

'Does it hurt a great deal?'

' 'Course it does! Hurts like hell and damnation!' cried Baggs, dashing the rest of the water over Reuben. 'Throbs like a blacksmith's hammer! Agony!'

'Sorry.' Reuben moved away, but Baggs called him back.

'No! Come here.' He studied Reuben's face. 'What did *you* do to me?'

'What do you mean?'

'*You!* You did something!' snarled Baggs. 'You started it last night, bringing that elder wood in, didn't you? Part of a ritual, I 'spect. I'm not as dumb as you think! And down by the river, you looked at me! Just before I tripped, you gave me such a look. That's what did it! It was witchcraft, wasn't it? You and those toads, in it together!'

'I swear!' gasped Reuben, nervously. 'I swear, I never did a single thing to hurt you.'

He tried to recall the sequence of events. He could hear the jangle of toad calls, see the arc made by the fishing line as it flicked through the air . . .

'You're doing it *now*! You're making it worse! That look! You're jealous of me and you're giving me that look! Go away! Get away!'

Once again Baggs searched around his neck for something that wasn't there, then, not finding it, he buried his face in the bedclothes. 'Don't come near!' he sobbed. 'Don't touch me, d'you hear? Witch's boy.'

Reuben backed away. 'It's not true, Baggs. I promise. I can't do anything. She wasn't a witch! She wasn't!'

'Baggs, hold your tongue,' said Flyte, appearing at the cottage door. 'Reuben, come here.'

Reuben was surprised when Flyte led him to the wagon and pulled open the curtains at the back. Every inch of the small inner space was crammed with stuff: leather cases, an iron box, plates hanging on the walls, books and pamphlets, herbs, bottles, brown paper packets.

'Keep your eyes off it!' Flyte warned him, handing Reuben two boxes of empty bottles. 'Carry that.' He followed with jars of powders and flasks of coloured liquid and set them out in the cottage on the big table by the window.

'Preparation. Production.'

'Yes, Doctor Flyte?'

'My Fantastic Formula!' Flyte let his fingers trail lovingly over the packets and bags on the table. His eyes gleamed. 'You will have the privilege – since Baggs is indisposed – of aiding me.'

Reuben experienced a peculiar sinking feeling in the middle of his body, as if whatever held his stomach in place had just let go. He wanted nothing to do with it. He knew the formula was useless. He felt he would never rid his head of the image of little George and his poor mother with the big sad eyes at Clodbury Fair; he'd sold them worthless rubbish!

Flyte lined the bottles and packets along the table. He opened some bags and breathed in their scents. He shook bottles and peered at labels. He was smiling.

'Boil the water. Get a measuring flask and some stirring rods.'

'It's my job,' moaned Baggs, rolling over on the mattress and attempting to focus his uncovered eye on them. 'Not his!'

Flyte ignored him. 'Reuben and me are just fine.'

Reuben suddenly had a terrible vision of his life with Flyte going on for ever. No Baggs. Just Reuben and Flyte. He could see himself standing at the back of the wagon, gesticulating as he addressed a large crowd – tricking them into buying the Fantastic Formula. A sea of pale and weary faces staring up at him, hopeful, pleading . . . A cold sweat broke out all over him.

I won't do it! I won't!

Flyte was watching Reuben, as if the pictures Reuben was seeing, he could see too. He licked his lip. A hissing noise escaped from his narrow lips.

'Reuben?' He began to unbuckle his broad leather belt, very slowly. 'Boy?'

Reuben bit his lip. 'Yes,' he said. 'Which first?' He picked up the nearest bottle. 'This one?'

Oh, he was a failure, a coward, a milksop . . .

'Aromatic spirits of ammonia!' said Flyte, uncorking a bottle. 'Smell!' He held it out for him.

Reuben sniffed, then staggered back, choking. 'Smelling salts!' He coughed.

'That'll give 'em something to think about,' chuckled Flyte.

'Yes, Doctor Flyte.'

Flyte used fennel to give the formula a good flavour. Hawkweed, fleawort and marjoram. Mint to make it smell good. He directed Reuben to steep the leaves in boiling water, stirring all the while. When all the flavour had been extracted, Reuben carefully strained the juice and poured the pale-green mixture into jugs; similar to the work he'd done with his grandmother, yet so different.

All afternoon, Reuben worked, filling the small green bottles with fresh formula. He was relieved to see that there was nothing harmful in the ingredients. Flyte had composed a fiery tasting brew which couldn't do any good – but nor could it harm.

As the light faded, Reuben sat beside the spluttering candle, writing labels for the bottles, using the lumpy grey ink that Flyte had made from chimney soot and water. It was the only time he'd ever regretted his grandmother teaching him the skill of writing.

'Tomorrow we will make some glue,' said Flyte. He sat beside the fire, watching Reuben at work. 'Useful, ain't he, eh, Baggs? Wish you could write like that, don't you, nincompoop?'

Baggs had spent the whole day resting on his mattress watching them as he drifted in and out of sleep. He pulled himself into a sitting position and farted loudly.

'That's what I think of the boy,' he said. 'So, what about the bad potion, Doctor?' He nodded towards Reuben. 'Is he doing that?'

'Not yet,' said Flyte.

Reuben went on scratching out the letters on the labels, listening carefully.

Flyte stood abruptly. 'Reuben – I know about Sarah Mearbeck. Heard how she cursed her cottage. How she changed you into a cat. How she used toads and spells to bring down her enemies . . .'

'She never–'

'Quiet,' said Flyte.

'Yeah, and what about the local, you know, whasisname? Magistrate? Don't want us to give you to him, do you? Or the churchwarden person? They'd send you back to Birtwell and you don't want that, do you?' put in Baggs.

Reuben took a big breath and waited.

'I want to know what you know,' said Flyte.

Reuben shook his head violently. 'No! She didn't show me anything you'd care about! Herbs and healing medicines, that's all!'

Flyte crept closer and closer, grabbed a handful of shirt below Reuben's chin and lifted the boy to his feet. 'A curse! A good, meaty, strong one.'

'I can't! I don't know how!'

Flyte threw him to the floor. 'Reuben, I've grown fond of you,' he said in a falsely sweet voice. He walked towards him. 'I don't want to hurt you, but . . .' Looking straight ahead, Flyte stepped directly on Reuben's knee as he spoke, pushing his weight against the bones, pressing and rolling them into the floor.

Reuben screamed as a fearful, sharp pain shot through him.

'I will! I will do it!' he cried.

Flyte removed his foot and Reuben scrabbled into the corner, rubbing his knee. 'Yes. I will!'

He couldn't help the tears running down his cheeks.

He knew Baggs was watching him, smirking, and he buried his head in his knees.

There's no such thing as curses, he wanted to say. You fool, Flyte; if I could make curses, you, Flyte, would get one. The biggest, most horrible, painful curse I could think of. You'd break out in warts as big as cabbages and pus-filled boils the size of potatoes and your nose would drop off and your eyes would spin like tops in their sockets and . . .

Flyte was watching him, eyes glinting dangerously. He showed his long teeth in a mirthless smile.

'Thinking of cursing me, too?' He laughed out loud. 'Baggs thinks you've done evil magic on him, but you can't touch me.'

He undid the laces at his shirt neck and took out the tiny, blue leather pouch which hung there. Immediately, Reuben thought of the satin purse that Meg Silver kept round her neck with her toad's leg talisman. But Flyte's lucky charm was a small brown stone. He tipped it onto his palm.

'A *real* toadstone,' Flyte said proudly.

'A *toad's stone?*'

'Don't play ignorant!' barked Flyte. ' 'Twas a toad your grandmother used to kill that old man! Right at your door!'

Reuben couldn't think of anything to say; whatever he said, Flyte wouldn't believe him.

Flyte was turning the stone over and over in his hands, as if it was the most marvellous thing in the world.

'Precious,' he smirked.

'Doctor Flyte's is the best sort,' Baggs told him. 'It's come from out of a toad's head, and it must have been a monster of an animal, from the size of it. The toad was killed at full moon, wasn't it, Doctor?' went on Baggs. 'That makes it extra strong and powerful.'

Flyte slipped the toadstone back into the bag. 'Nothing can harm me.' He patted the little bag. 'No hexes. No curses, spells. Nothing.'

'I haven't got one,' said Baggs in a small voice. 'And you hate me,' he said to Reuben. 'That's why you can work your magic on me. I've lost my toadstone but I'm going to get me one soon. I will.'

Reuben looked from one to the other, thinking.

There *was* the strange coincidence of the toads croaking down at the river, just as Baggs hurt himself.

There was that odd behaviour of the toad outside the cottage, the leaping toad.

The toad stain on the baby.

Perhaps it did all mean something? . . . But no, it couldn't! Granny said toads were interesting creatures. We watched them. They don't do anything wrong. They're not evil.

Nor am I. Nor do I have any powers. But, perhaps . . .

'A curse?' said Reuben, as if he'd finally come round to agreeing to do it.

'Ah, ha! That's it!' Flyte said.

'Will you call up a little devil? Do you speak to imps?' asked Baggs. 'It's got to be strong.'

'Potent. Dark and dangerous. Deadly. A curse to end all curses,' said Flyte.

'If anyone found out, I'd be hanged like my grandmother!' cried Reuben.

'Nah. We won't tell a soul,' said Doctor Flyte, winking at Baggs. 'No one will know but us.'

15
Reuben's Root Man

Flyte must have the fingers of a pickpocket – lighter than air, thought Reuben, waking next morning and finding his ankles and hands had been tied up again without him feeling a thing.

He glanced across at Baggs, who was sleeping deeply; his injury had exhausted him.

'Shall we go?' Flyte appeared quietly at the door. 'We've got to find that evil herb, eh? Mystical root? Whatever you need for your curse.' He quickly untied Reuben.

Reuben had been pondering what to do. I *could* make a poison, he thought. There are plenty of dangerous herbs – roots and toadstools too – that I could use, but I can't! I can't hurt someone I don't even know. Who probably isn't even bad! So what *can* I do? Finally, he had decided to look for a plant that Flyte didn't recognise; something safe, make up some sort of incantation to please them and then add the stuff to a bottle of Flyte's formula.

And by the time he finds out I've tricked him, I'll be gone, he thought. I'll have to be!

Flyte led the way through the woods, Reuben followed.

Sunshine rained down in sharp beams, illuminating

the ground in patches. There were few flowers at this time of year; Reuben spotted some white blackthorn blossom on the bare branches of the bush and some pale pink flowers of the butterbur. Its leaves were hardly developed. Reuben smiled, remembering how he used to be sent to collect them when they grew as broad as plates, then his grandmother would wrap up pats of butter in them to keep it fresh.

Sweet violet, wood sorrel and wood anemone – none were flowering. It was because of the late frost. What am I going to use? he wondered. There must be something. There must be!

'Fox,' said Flyte, as he glimpsed an animal slipping in and out of the trees far ahead. It was hard to be sure what it was, staring into the sun, but Reuben recognised Shadow. She was still watching him. Protecting him. His Shadow was always there.

Reuben pushed on further into the woods. Flyte slashed at the bushes and leaves with a stick. His jacket caught on the twigs and brambles. He stumbled and swore.

'Reuben, I don't like walking.'

'It's only March, or maybe April by now,' Reuben reminded him. 'There isn't much out yet. I'm looking for . . .' He paused, wondering. Because, if Flyte knew his herbs, he'd recognise whatever Reuben picked. And Reuben had to get something to trick him.

'Here's aconite,' said Reuben, carefully.

'For rat bites,' snapped Flyte. 'Did I say my victim's bit by a rat?'

'No. Where did you study, Doctor Flyte?' Reuben added.

'Study?'

'I mean to be a doctor. If I were a gentleman I'd be a doctor. Did you go to London? Is it a wonderful town? There's a place called the Royal Society in London, this man told my grandmother all about it, and all these clever men go there and talk about the stars and microscopes – that's an instrument to see small things with, and–'

'Be silent!' Flyte swiped him with his stick.

'Ow!' He's an ignorant quack, thought Reuben, rubbing his leg. I'll fool him. I need a plant with large roots.

There! He stopped and pulled at the new leaves of an emerging plant, deep in the shadowy undergrowth.

'What's that?' asked Flyte.

'Scrophularia,' said Reuben, holding his breath. Did Flyte know it?

'I know it,' said Flyte, looking at him haughtily.

'You know, then, that the plant is governed by the moon,' said Reuben. 'And that it cures the King's evil, but the root is what I want.'

Reuben dug away until the lumpy, knotty roots came up in his hand.

'Looks like a parsnip,' said Flyte in disgust.

'No, no,' Reuben assured him. Inwardly he was exhilarated. Flyte knew nothing! 'This is a very powerful root. You'll see.' He dusted the earth off it. 'See how it has lumps, like arms? Tendrils like legs? Granny called it Old Man's Root. I can make a powerful, strong spell with this.'

'Hah! You'd better be right, Reuben, or else.'

Reuben smiled to himself. Yes, he'd better be right or else he was going to find himself tossed in the ditch with his throat cut, that was certain.

When they returned to the cottage, Baggs had lit a fire and was boiling water for tea.

'I'm well now, Doctor,' he told them cheerfully. 'See, I can help now. Back on my feet.'

'About time,' said Flyte. 'Reuben's got something for the spell. Let's see what he does with it.'

Reuben carefully washed the mud off the root and dried it beside the fire. The swollen root was perfect; it couldn't have looked more like a tiny, wizened old man than a tiny, wizened old man himself.

'I need you to describe the victim,' said Reuben. 'Age, height, that sort of thing.'

'I'll be damned if I know such details!' snapped Flyte. 'He's an interfering hypocrite, I can tell you that.'

'He's a doctor,' Baggs added. 'He thinks he's clever. A gentleman, too. He wanted us run out of town last year–'

'And this time, God willing, I shall have *him* run out – in a coffin!' said Flyte.

'What did he do?'

'Said the Doctor's formula was nothing but coloured water!' said Baggs. 'Accused him of being a quack and a – a – what was that other thing, Doctor?'

'A charlatan!' growled Flyte.

'I see.' Reuben tried to keep his face impassive. 'Do you want my curse to kill him or just harm him?'

'Kill,' said Flyte, closing his eyes and smiling. Then his eyes snapped open. 'But not immediately. An hour or so, after we've left, even a day would suffice.'

Reuben nodded.

He took the clean, dry root and made three small incisions in the head. He pressed three tiny fennel seeds into the cuts, making a face. Then he took the root outside and laid it on the flat tree stump.

Baggs and Flyte watched his every move.

Reuben placed elder leaves – since Baggs was so scared of them – around the root in an intricate pattern, lacing them over each other and muttering to himself as he did so. Next he dropped leaves of the wood spurge onto the root, letting them float down over it like snow. Then he walked around the stone three times clockwise, three times anticlockwise, three times clockwise again.

Flyte watched him through narrowed eyes.

'Nine is the number,' Reuben said mysteriously,

remembering the superstitious chantings of the village children. Nine was always regarded as a most important, powerful number.

Flyte chewed nervously on the end of his pipe. 'Go on, go on.'

'Now.' Reuben stood poised beside the effigy of the little man, with a handful of thorns and small sharp twigs. 'I need his name.'

'Brittlebank,' said Flyte through clenched teeth.

'Kill!' Reuben stabbed a thorn into the root-man's head. 'Agony!' He pushed a miniature stick through the root-man's heart. 'Dead! Brittlebank be gone!' he hissed.

Flyte twitched and cringed as the root-man was struck through.

Reuben muttered some magical-sounding words while he cut off a tiny segment of root and taking the cork from a bottle of Flyte's Fantastic Formula, he dropped the bit of root into it.

'Done!' said Reuben. 'Be careful of that bottle of potion. It's very dangerous.'

Flyte nodded.

Flyte was so preoccupied he wasn't aware of Reuben looking at him. He held the small bottle up to his face to study it. He grinned, a smile that for once involved his eyes; the whole of his twisted, lopsided face came alive – with malice.

'Keep it with you at all times,' said Reuben. 'Hate it.

The potion will grow stronger and more potent the more you channel your anger and hatred into it.'

And that I know for the truth, thought Reuben, because the more I despise you, Doctor Flyte, the deeper and wilder my hatred grows!

16
The Toadstone Man

Baggs was improved enough by the afternoon to sit outside the cottage in the sun. He took off his boots and grey wool stockings and aired his dirty toes in the sunshine.

'Bring me some drink. I'll have two oatcakes and bacon, if there is some still,' he said to Reuben. 'I'm ravenous, though my head hurts – feels like I've been kicked in the face by old Nellie.'

Before Reuben could get the food, Flyte stood suddenly and pointed.

'Well, well! Here he is!' A grin spread over his face. 'Mister Pepperday. At last!' He walked up the path to meet the man who was ambling down between the trees towards them.

The first thing Reuben noticed about Mister Pepperday was the vast wicker basket tied to his back with wide, leather straps. It was shaped like an egg, almost as big as the little man, reaching nearly to the ground and jutting up above his narrow shoulders.

'Good afternoon!' he called, unbuckling the basket and setting it down in front of the cottage, and rubbing at his shoulders. 'Mighty heavy,' he said, grinning a black hole of a grin since he had so few teeth. 'Some ale wouldn't go amiss after that journey, Doctor Flyte.'

Baggs kicked Reuben. Reuben went to get the ale. The large barrel tied to the underside of the wagon was nearly empty and the brew was cloudy and stale-tasting, but Mister Pepperday drank it thirstily.

'What's happened to you, Master Baggs?'

'Fishing hook,' said Baggs. 'It were his fault,' he added, pointing at Rueben. 'I'm glad you're here, Pepperday. Good timing, that is.'

'Flyte's Formula not helping?'

Baggs laughed. 'Nah! It's a stone I'm needing.'

'Of course.' Mister Pepperday opened the top of the basket. 'I've brought you some fresh food, too,' he said, taking out some cheese and dark, knobbly bread. 'Thought you'd be needing some. And plenty of stones. And those stones is heavy.'

He heaved a large leather pouch from the basket. 'Give us a cloth to lay them on.'

Baggs lay a piece of blue fabric on the ground and Mister Pepperday tipped the contents of the leather bag onto it.

Reuben edged forward. He was expecting jewels. Rubies and diamonds, shining things. His heart sank when he saw these were ordinary stone-coloured smooth stones, just like Doctor Flyte's toadstone.

Pepperday, noticing Reuben watching closely, handed

him one of the brown pebbles, none of which was bigger than a man's thumbnail.

'See how they're shaped like toads?' said Mister Pepperday, grinning at him. 'The head there. Back legs there?'

'Perhaps . . .'

The stone was shaped like an arrowhead and humped just like a toad's back. He could almost make out the long, rounded back legs tucked in and the wide mouth. He picked up another. They were all similar although with some it was less easy to make out the toad shape. They were patterned just like the mottling of toad skin; greens and browns, yellow and black. A heap of tiny toads!

'Ever heard of Shakespeare?' asked Pepperday.

Reuben nodded his head. Everyone knew Shakespeare. His grandmother had even been able to quote a passage from a sonnet.

'He was the nation's greatest poet,' said Pepperday. 'Listen . . .' And he recited the few lines in a dramatic voice.

'Sweet are the uses of adversity,
Which like the toad, ugly and venomous,
Wears yet a precious jewel in its head.

'And that,' he added, pointing at the stone, 'is the jewel!'

'Shakespeare meant that?' asked Reuben.

'Yes indeed. It's the most powerful part of the animal. Magical,' went on Mister Pepperday. 'Any part of the body that's been envenomed or hurt can be cured with just a touch of one of these little things.'

'Well – put it on Baggs's cheek then,' said Reuben swiftly. 'Let's see it working.'

Silence fell.

There! He'd got them! He'd trapped them! He found himself suddenly standing taller, defiant. He was right. Why did they believe these superstitious tales?

Then Baggs burst out laughing. So did Mister Pepperday.

'Oh, lad,' said Pepperday, 'you are as ignorant as a babe, are you not?'

Reuben stared at them, bewildered. 'Why are you laughing?'

Baggs laughed again, then winced, his hand cupping his sore face. 'See, Skinny, the thing is, them ain't actually *real* toadstones. They're dug out of the ground, down in Dorsetshire.'

'What are they then?' Reuben asked.

'They're just bits of old fish, mostly. That's what I was told. Fish *teeth* I believe,' said Mister Pepperday. 'Fossilised. Though how the fishes got themselves on land, I don't know.' He shook his head.

'It was long ago,' said Flyte.

'And some are just pebbles from the beach,' said

Pepperday, winking. 'I know, because I picked them up myself.' He laughed. 'Not real toadstones. The *real* toadstones are hard to find and particularly expensive. You'd pay guineas for them – like Flyte did for his, 'cos I got that from a foreign gentleman, so you can be sure I paid a lot.'

'It's not right!' Reuben blurted out, angrily. 'It's quackery! Fakes!'

Flyte slapped his knee and chuckled.

'Little boy,' Pepperday said, smiling, 'what do you care?'

Reuben rolled a toadstone round and round in his fingers. Useless, worthless stone. Why should he care? But he did because he knew his grandmother would and she'd be so angry at such ignorance, and profiting from ignorance.

'What about the stone you have, Doctor Flyte?' he asked, daringly. 'Won't that mend Baggs's face?'

'No.'

'They don't work for no one 'cept the owner,' said Baggs. 'If Doctor Flyte tried to heal someone with it, it wouldn't like it, and would stop keeping him safe.'

'Never a moment's illness since I bought it,' added Flyte.

Baggs fingered his bandaged cheek. 'I do need another of my own,' he said.

'You'll have the best stone I've got, Baggs,' said Pepperday.

Baggs grinned smugly at Reuben. 'I'll get better then, you'll see and you won't be able to touch me again, witch's boy.'

'But how do you *know* the stone's real?' asked Reuben.

Baggs looked aggrieved. 'Because of the cost, you ignorant duffer. The more you pay, the more real it must be!'

Money changed hands, and later that afternoon, Mister Pepperday left them with a much lighter basket on his back.

Reuben was sorry when he'd gone. Without Pepperday an air of gloom and suspicion quickly descended.

He trudged down to the river to fill the big wooden bucket with water. Baggs could have done it, but he was sitting with his feet up, smoking and playing with his new stone.

Rueben felt Flyte's eyes on his back as he pushed through the bushes to where the river ran deepest, as sure as if they'd been pinned to his leather jerkin.

I'm not going anywhere, Flyte, he told him silently. I'm not going to run. Not yet. But first real chance I get, I will.

He knelt by the river and washed his face and hands. The water was icy cold, clear and fresh. A sudden splash made him look up.

'Shadow!'

The big dog stood a few feet away in the water, her bedraggled tail wagging slowly. Her bright, clever eyes stared into his.

Reuben held out his hand, wishing he'd brought a scrap of food for her.

'Come, come!' he whispered.

The dog stood and watched him for a whole minute, until at last she moved tentatively towards him, tail swinging, ears low. Her dull fur was matted and full of twigs, dried mud and burrs. She looked thinner than ever.

Reuben waited as she came nearer, afraid that if he put out his hand or moved, she'd take fright and run. At last she was close enough to touch. Reuben stretched out his arm and ran his fingers gently over her head and ears, murmuring endearments. The dog crept closer and closer until Reuben found he had his arms around her wet, shaggy body and was hugging her tightly. He felt her beating heart against his own. Her sour, dead-meat smell filled his nostrils and suddenly he remembered the night, just a few days ago – though it felt like years – when he'd slept so warmly beneath the wagon and woken to that gut-wrenching, rotten smell. It was the dog! Shadow must have slept beside him all night! Now the dreadful smell was wonderful and he buried his face in her rough fur and sobbed.

'You fine, splendid creature,' he told her. 'Beautiful

hound with the fastest legs and the bravest heart. Faithful friend. When we're free, I shall wash you and brush you and feed you till your coat gleams and your eyes shine and you bark with joy!'

The last person he'd hugged like this was his granny.

He couldn't help himself now from remembering again the feel of his arms around his grandmother, just like this, feeling the last warmth of her touch.

He remembered what he'd been trying, ever since, to forget.

17
The Hanging

It was his grandmother's last night.

Reuben sat outside the barn that was serving as her temporary gaol. He pulled the moth-eaten, ragged old coat round his stomach. The ground was hard as iron and freezing cold beneath him and his back ached from leaning against the wooden door.

Sarah Mearbeck whispered through the locked door. Her voice was weak. 'It's wrong of me to ask – it's not fair of me to – but I'm an old woman, and God forgive me, I'm weak . . .' She broke off, wheezing and trying to get her breath. 'I'm scared, Reuben, I didn't want to admit it to you, I wanted to be strong, but . . .'

'Yes?' He turned and put his lips close to the gaps in the wood.

'I dream about it, the moment when they pull the wheels out from under my feet. I'm so light now, Reuben, no more than a bag of flour. I'll struggle and kick on the end of the rope – I won't go peaceful. I'll flap around like a bird, trying to die, and I won't die because I'm too light . . .' She choked and stopped.

Reuben could hear her trying to stifle her sobs. 'What do you want me to do?'

'Reuben, this is hard for me to ask – it will be the hardest thing that you will ever have to do.'

'What? What is it?'

His grandmother spoke quickly, anxious to get the words out. 'I want you to hold on to me. Hold on to my legs, and pull like you're trying to drag the whole world down. Pull so I've got extra weight and die quickly. And just keep holding until you don't feel any movement. Till I'm dead.'

Tears welled up in Reuben's eyes, spilled down his cheeks. Without sniffing, without his voice breaking, he said softly, 'Yes, I will. If you want me to, I will.'

'Ah! Dear Reuben! There, I feel better already. Why, Reuben, if I can't pass away peacefully in my bed with you holding my hand, then the next best thing will be this, feeling your arms around my legs.'

'Oh, Granny! Dear Granny,' he said, picturing it, imagining it and hating it.

'The last thing I'll know won't be the hangman's noose, won't be kicking at the air, won't be anything, except – my dear Reuben's arms around me.'

And she started to sing. Her voice was so weak, it was no more than a rasping, tremulous whisper. Reuben joined in.

'There lies a knight slain under his shield,
With a downnnn . . .
His hounds they lie down at his feet,

So well they do their master keep.

With a down, derry, derry, derry down, down.'

If only we had hounds to lie down at our feet and keep us safe and warm. To go on guarding us even when we're dead, thought Reuben.

Now it was late afternoon, light was fading, the surrounding houses were beginning to disappear into the gloom. The trial had been short, and Reuben sensed that everything had been dealt with very quickly, almost as if the makeshift jury were worried they might be stopped by some interfering person if they didn't hurry. If only he'd had the power to insist they wait for a real magistrate's hearing.

They'll come and take her soon, thought Reuben, and there's nothing I can do. He shivered inside the old coat the innkeeper had lent him. He was so stiff his legs and arms felt as though they were made from wood. But it doesn't matter, thought Reuben, it doesn't matter. Soon all be over.

They came for her.

They had to help her out of the barn, she was so weak. But not too weak to put her arms around Reuben and hug him one last time. He vowed to remember exactly the feel of those thin arms holding him tight. Like a precious cage. The safest place on earth.

Then they led her away.

'Keep that mind of yours curious,' she whispered to

him, never thinking of herself. 'Turn away from the dark. Be true to yourself. I love you, little Reuben.'

Reuben couldn't look too closely at her. Her face was so worn and tired and pitiful. Her hair was knotted, hanging around her face in dirty locks. Where was the blue cloth she wound around her head? Her fresh white collar?

He helped her go towards the small group at the gallows.

'It's all right, dear boy, don't care,' she whispered. 'Don't be sad for me.'

The small crowd was quiet and shifted nervously as she approached.

Reuben closed his eyes against the dangling noose. He looked only at the small, wooden trolley that they would remove from beneath her, leaving her hanging by the rope.

That's when Reuben would dart out and grab her and pull.

The words of the righteous villagers, the monotonous drone of the magistrate, passed over his head in a blur.

Finally, when she was in place, held up by two burly men, Reuben managed to meet her eyes and hold her stare.

All Reuben was watching was his grandmother and she watched only him.

The church man spoke a few words; they meant

nothing to Reuben, as far as he was concerned God and everyone else had abandoned them. Another man placed the rope around her neck. What a coarse, thick rope for such a delicate, stalk-like neck. A ribbon would have served.

'Granny?'

She smiled at him. 'I'm with you always, Reuben,' she whispered.

They pushed the trolley out from below her.

Reuben ran forward. 'Granny!'

He jumped at her, wrapped his arms around her, swinging and pulling on her with every ounce of strength he had left . . .

18
Toads Again

In the early evening, after Mister Pepperday's visit, Flyte and Baggs sat huddled together outside, drinking the last of the ale. Flyte was rolling his bone dice over and over on the tree stump, Baggs was plucking two wood pigeons they'd trapped. The birds' feathers lay scattered like snowflakes.

Perhaps the ale had become stronger as it settled in the barrel, Reuben thought, because the two of them were growing louder and louder.

'Come listen to this, Reuben,' Baggs called.

Reuben went out cautiously. 'Are you better, Baggs?' he ventured.

'Yes! Told you my toadstone would work, didn't I?' He fondled his new charm which now nestled against his neck encased in a brown bag.

Baggs's bandages made his head look enormous and it seemed to Reuben that Baggs found his new, larger head too heavy to hold up comfortably. It rolled and drooped, as if Baggs hadn't the strength to keep it upright. His eyes were bright and feverish and Reuben saw how Baggs's fingers kept missing their mark as they tried to rip off the birds' feathers.

'We've thought of something,' said Baggs.

'*I've* thought of something,' Flyte corrected him. 'You need a brain to think something, Baggs.'

Baggs laughed, but Flyte's words had wiped the smile from his mouth and his eyes went flat and sad.

'Yesterday – toadstones – that's what put it in mind,' went on Flyte. 'Reuben, you're to become a toad eater.'

'Toad eater? What . . .?'

Flyte and Baggs laughed.

'Yes, little stick-boy,' said Baggs. He sat up straight, but it seemed an awful effort and he sighed and flopped again. 'Toad eater. You can prove the Doctor's formula is real strong – by eating a toad and living to tell the tale!' Baggs licked his lips and grinned sloppily at Reuben. 'I'm sure they taste lovely!'

'I can't – I won't,' Reuben said in a small voice. 'I won't do it. Nobody eats toads. They're poisonous!'

'Ah, Reuben, you're wrong,' said Doctor Flyte, draining off the rest of his ale. 'You will. Because I say you will.'

'You can't make me!' cried Reuben, knowing this wasn't true.

Flyte gave him a meaningful glance. 'I can. I'll tell about the terrible curse you put on poor Baggs, or – well, there's plenty of ways!'

'I never put a curse on him!' Reuben glanced from one to the other. They had him fixed, between them, with their stares. He gulped for breath. 'I can't . . . Not *eat* one – I'd die!'

'Oh, oh,' Baggs groaned, suddenly. 'I feel ill.' He dropped the pigeons on the grass, clasped his head in his hands and rocked backwards and forwards. 'My head! Worse and worse! The moment *he* speaks to me – I'm sick!'

Baggs's lips were pale, his skin glistened with sweat, his hands trembled.

'It wasn't me–' Reuben tried to say. 'I can't–'

'Shove off. Leave me be.' Baggs pushed past Reuben and staggered into the cottage. They heard him crash onto the floor.

Flyte picked up the pigeon that Baggs had dropped, and tossed it to Reuben.

'Finish this. And when they're done, cook them. It'll only be you and me eating and it's just as well, not much meat on a pigeon, this time of year.'

Flyte was right about Baggs; he did not move from his mattress all evening, not to eat, drink or speak.

That night Reuben lay beside Doctor Flyte. As usual Flyte had tied his feet and hands together and the other end of the rope was wrapped around Flyte's hands so any movement that Reuben made would wake him too.

Reuben stared through the darkness towards the door.

Maybe I could get free if I was careful, but how would I climb over Flyte? Flyte'll wake. He'll hear the door.

He'll sense it. I don't dare. Or is it that I'm such a coward and daren't go in the night, in the dark, alone in the woods?

Flyte wants me to try and escape, to give him an excuse to flog me, no doubt. I must get away, but . . . Fear of being caught by Flyte, and the ropes around him, held him there. Flyte would beat him, taunt him, punish him the way he'd already described, he was sure he would. No, he had to have a better plan than just running out into the forest at night.

Sometime before dawn, Reuben woke. Baggs was making a terrible noise, crying, moaning and tossing from side to side, thrashing his arms around and rocking his head backwards and forwards. Odd, rough, words fell from his mouth like broken things.

Poison!

Baggs's wound had gone bad.

'Shut your noise!' Flyte roared, turning over and covering his head with his arms.

Reuben lay back and stared up at the ceiling. Baggs thinks I did it. A charm or a spell. The particular way I looked at him, but it wasn't me! It wasn't! No!

By daybreak, Baggs was clutching at his face, ripping at the bandages as if they were nails piercing his skin. His heels beat on the floor. Shivers wracked his body. He wept and wailed but his words made no sense.

When Flyte woke he untied Reuben without a word.

He took one look at Baggs then went outside, slamming the door behind him so hard that bits of the walls came down in chunks.

'Shut him up! I don't want to hear that noise. Shut him up, Reuben!' he called.

Reuben knelt down beside the mattress and laid his hand on Baggs's brow. His skin was red and burning hot with fever.

Oh, Lord! It was bad, really bad. Reuben scrunched himself back in his corner and chewed on his fingernails.

What did Granny do when this happened? He knocked his head on the wall, trying to beat the memories back into his brain. What did she used to do? Though I haven't the herbs she had, thought Reuben, so even if I did remember, what use would it be?

She hadn't believed in letting blood.

'*Reuben*,' he seemed to hear her say, '*what can be wise in the barber-surgeon letting all that fine red stuff out? What if he lets some good out, along with the bad, by mistake?*'

She had told him about a man called Harvey, who claimed the blood went round and round in the body. That the heart pumped it. But everyone knew it flowed down to the fingers and toes.

Should I try and bleed him? Reuben wondered. I've seen it done many times, just a small cut into the vein, a sharp knife . . .

'Help me, help me, I'm so cold.'

'Shh, shh!' Reuben glanced to the door but there was no sign of Flyte. Baggs's shivers were so violent he almost shook himself off the mattress. 'Hush, Baggs. Not so noisy.'

He squatted beside him and covered him with all the linen and bits of clothing and rugs he could find. Two minutes later Baggs threw them off, swearing and complaining of the heat.

Reuben returned to his corner to think. Granny. Granny, tell me what to do. If he dies they'll think I did it. He mustn't die!

'Well?' asked Flyte, appearing in the doorway.

'Bad,' said Reuben. 'He's got a fever.'

Flyte looked outside, down the hill towards the river.

'He's a muttonhead,' he said, dolefully.

'But–'

'Always has been. Bone idle, gormless dolt!'

'Don't you care at all?' cried Reuben. 'He's your friend! Surely you can do something! Don't you know any *good* medicine?'

Flyte lunged and caught Reuben up by his jerkin.

'What are you trying to say?' he spat in his face. 'Think I'm no good as a doctor?'

'I–'

'People look at me with respect, Reuben. I've got a reputation. Baggs is nothing. Alive or dead. It doesn't matter.'

'I think–'

'Don't care what you think. Understand? And I don't care about Baggs.'

'Yes,' said Reuben.

'The next fair. That's what I care about. We must plan this toad eating scam with great care. Skullduggery is a dangerous game to play.' He grinned and clapped his hands together gleefully. 'And I like danger, I like such trickery!'

Reuben stared out of the window, afraid to let Flyte see his expression in case he gave anything away. 'Yes, Doctor Flyte.'

His eyes smarted with unshed tears. His body was tensed with unspent energy. Such an anger was burning up inside him. Such a hatred. He imagined it flaming up from his feet, engulfing him in red-hot heat. Yellow and orange flames would be dancing in his eyes if Flyte chanced to look into them.

I don't care about Baggs, why should I? thought Reuben. But I shan't leave him, I can't. Just to spite you, Flyte, I'll try my best to save him.

19
Toad Eater

'This'll be a great trick!' Flyte cracked his hand on his thigh. 'Reuben, toad eater! Though it'll only be a bit of bread. We'll fashion the dough to look like a toad.'

This information was a relief to Reuben. He couldn't die from eating dough.

'Yes, Doctor Flyte.' Wearily, Reuben took the lid off the wooden flour box that Flyte handed him and peered inside. 'It's full of weevils.'

'Good. Weevils'll give it texture,' said Flyte. 'Go on, put it on the table and mix it up with some water. Know how to make dough?'

Reuben nodded. He poured the flour in a heap on the table and watched as the brown weevils began furiously burrowing back into the dark interior of the soft pile. I'd rather eat acorn flour, like we did one hard winter, than eat this weevily stuff, he thought. Still, they'll be dead when they're cooked – it was when they wiggled around in your mouth that they were so unpleasant.

He made a well in the centre and poured in some water, then, mixing with his fingers, he produced a lump of speckled, pliable dough.

'That'll do. Here, let me.' Silently Flyte began to form

the dough into separate bits of toad shape. 'Won't matter greatly what they look like,' said Flyte, rolling the dough over the table. 'We'll get them coloured like toad skin. There's pigments in the wagon, left over from the painted notices. You'll be up on the cart – no one will see too well.'

The completed toad shapes – a batch of legs with wide, webbed feet and arms with tiny fingers – were set beside the fire to cook and harden.

'Come now, Reuben, you can smile. This will be a great trick! The audience will see you eat a toad's leg, see you fall down nearly dead, then I'll bring you back to life again! A spectacle!'

Reuben nodded, not trusting himself to speak. If you only knew what I really think, what I really feel, he thought, gripping the table edge, you wouldn't ask me to smile! Trickery and deception! I want no part of it!

Flyte went out to his tree trunk and settled down to smoke his pipe.

Reuben sat on the doorstep, listened to the rushing water, to the toads still calling from the river and the chirping and cawing of the birds. Granny would have been happy here. He pictured the two of them living in the cottage, safe from the likes of Meg Silver: cooking, making brews, sitting beside the fire with Shadow . . .

Now's the moment to escape, Reuben told himself. If I really wanted to, I could. Shadow's waiting, down by the water. We could outrun Flyte. We'd be at the top of the hill and hiding up a tree in minutes. Flyte'd never find me. Baggs can't chase me . . . But that was the problem. Baggs.

Suddenly, as if he knew Reuben was thinking about him, Baggs let out a terrible shriek and sat up. Keeled over. Screamed.

Flyte gave Reuben a narrow-eyed look. 'Shut him up!'

Reuben ran to Baggs. It was a terrible sight. Baggs's face was worse – a swollen pulpy mass, like an overripe fruit about to burst its skin.

He couldn't leave Baggs. It would be cheating. Without me, Baggs'll die. And I shan't let Flyte have that pleasure. No, Reuben told himself. I'll wait. As soon as Baggs is better, then I'll go.

If he got better.

If Baggs didn't recover, if he died, Flyte would bind Reuben to his side, body and soul. He'd never get away. Maybe, he mused, Baggs was just a replacement for a previous boy Flyte'd picked up, who'd died. Certainly Flyte had no feelings for him. Next it would be Reuben who wore the eye patch and pretended to have the stones. Reuben, who sat beside Flyte smoking the pipe and telling jokes. Reuben, who would never quite have the strength to leave, never quite be daring enough, be stuck here till he died . . . For ever and ever and ever.

He shivered.

I will go, Reuben promised himself. I'll get away somehow, just as soon as Baggs is better. So Baggs must get better, he must!

All through the day Baggs battled with the fever. It was as if a fearsome visitor sat by his head, whispering terrible tales into his ear. Baggs twisted away from the awful voice, shouted at it, tried to hit it, but still the mysterious, invisible person sat there, cursing him, poisoning him.

Reuben watched his tortured sleep, wishing he could help. Granny had used an ointment of alkanet. Alkanet! Where could he get that? And St Peter's wort – you crushed the leaves and laid it on the sore, but he had none. Willow bark, everyone knew that a willow-bark infusion brought down the fever.

I could go and look for some herbs, Reuben thought, but that frost did for most things, I know.

Baggs's cries gathered into a high-pitched scream. Flyte burst into the cottage, pressing his hands over his ears.

'Stop him!' he yelled. 'I'll kill him if he keeps this up. There's no peace. Make him stop!'

'What shall I do?'

'Shut him up. Just for pity's sake shut him up.'

'All right. I'll try. I need willow bark.'

Reuben ran down to the river where willow trees hung over the water, their roots tangling and twisting in the muddy bank. He used a pointed stick to rip off some bark and took it back to the cottage. Quickly he boiled up the old black kettle and poured the hot water over the bark.

'This'll help, Baggs. This'll bring the fever down.'

While the bark infusion strengthened, he rummaged through Flyte's bags of herbs and bottles of powders and, to his delight, found St John's wort and horsetail, both of which he added to his concoction. All the while, Flyte leaned against the door jamb, watching him, a strange smile twisting his lips.

When the mixture was ready, and cooled, Reuben knelt beside Baggs and forced some of the medicine through his clenched lips with a small spoon.

Baggs's face now looked more like a giant, red pumpkin than a head. Both his eyes were puffy, bruised and closed tight. The spots and pimples that plagued his face had multiplied like bubbles of soup coming up to boil, their fiery, glistening, yellow heads ready to explode. They had erupted all over his neck, too – were even creeping under his grey, bloodstained shirt – even popping out in patches on the backs of his hands.

Baggs swallowed the drink without opening his eyes. He choked a bit, then swallowed again.

'Good, good,' whispered Reuben.

What was worrying Reuben most, at the moment, was the smell. It was bad. He had to look under that bandage. Carefully, he began to unwind the dirty cloth. The more he took off, the stronger the smell, until the stench hit him like a solid wall, the most terrible smell of flyblown meat, old vegetables and cesspits. He twisted away, retching, gagging and gasping for fresh air. He stumbled to the door, gulping at the fresh air, like a drowning man.

Flyte stepped out of his way, laughing at him. 'Not very sweet, eh? Well, Baggs never was.'

Reuben gritted his teeth. Bracing himself, holding his breath, he went back and knelt beside Baggs. The last scrap of cloth, stained yellow with pus, dark brown with blood, had dried to his cheek.

Holding his breath, sobbing with revulsion, Reuben eased off a corner of the bandage. Baggs squealed and hit out at him, but Reuben pushed him back and quickly ripped off the final strand of bandage and tossed it onto the fire.

The wound was a festering, stinking mess: yellow, purple and red.

Reuben sat back on his haunches and stared at it. It was way beyond anything he'd seen before. Even his grandmother had never . . .

And he remembered. Tall John's arm! A boulder had fallen on it, not broken it, but split the skin and it had gone really stinking like this and they'd all said he'd lose his arm, but no, his grandmother had saved it. With bread! A poultice of old bread, that's what she'd put on it. And the arm had mended.

'Then I will, too!' he cried.

'What's that?' said Flyte. He was standing in the doorway, watching them.

'Nothing. Talking to my granny, that's all.' Reuben bit his lip. For a moment he'd really thought his grandmother was there.

Reuben found a bit of bread at the bottom of a barrel, just how he wanted it to be; damp and furred with a green-blue dusty mould, which came off on his fingers.

'*Yes, yes*', his grandmother said to him. '*Well done. That's the stuff. Try it. Go on.*'

'What are you doing?' said Flyte.

Reuben jumped.

Flyte had crept into the room and was standing inches behind him staring at Baggs, unemotionally, as if he didn't really see him at all.

'Baggs is worse,' said Reuben. 'I'm making a poultice.'

'He's going to croak,' said Flyte, flatly. 'Nuisance.'

Did he mean Baggs was a nuisance? Or his death would be?

'Can I try this?' Reuben cast about for something to convince him. 'It's a magic Granny used,' he said quickly. 'Witchcraft.'

Flyte's face twitched, then broke into a satisfied smile.

'I knew you'd do something in the end, Reuben,' he said slowly. 'You and the Devil are good friends, eh? If that boy lives I'll surely trust that other potion you've made me. Who'd have thought you'd want to save Baggs? Go on, then. Make it good, mind.'

Reuben pushed the jagged edges of the gash together as well as he could, then dampened the old bread with a bit of water and lay it tenderly, green side down, over the wound, before binding it all up again tightly with a fresh cloth.

There was nothing else he could do now, except wait.

20
A Terrible Shock

The longest day of Reuben's life had been the day before they hanged his grandmother. That day, time had been so stretched, so achingly slow, that he thought it would never end. And this day was nearly as bad.

Reuben sat beside Baggs, bathing his face, mopping his brow, dribbling water into his mouth and soothing him through the worst of his nightmares.

'Don't bother,' said Flyte, laying out the dirty cards on the table in a game of patience. 'He'll die. When a wound goes yellow, there's nothing you can do. Seen it many times.'

Reuben didn't reply.

He stared at Baggs's bandaged, bruised face. Was it less red? Was it less swollen? Please, please work, he begged. Then I can go! I'll be free!

'Only way that'll mend is with help from the Devil,' said Flyte with a wink. 'So, if he survives, we'll know who your accomplice is, Reuben, won't we?'

Outside the cottage, a bird suddenly began to squawk loudly and raucously. Flyte leaped to the doorway. 'Look! In the beech tree!' he pointed for Reuben to see. 'A magpie! *One for sorrow*, hey, Reuben? *Two for joy*. Nope, there's only the one. A timely sign, by God! No hope for the lad now, even the magpie knows Baggs is going to kick the bucket.'

Reuben stared at the black and white bird as it jumped jauntily through the branches of the tree. Was it really foretelling Baggs's death? He threw a stone towards it and the bird flew off, cawing crossly.

'A bleak portent!' said Flyte, grinning. 'Your magic bread will have to be strong to beat that!'

Everyone knew that the arrival of a bird cawing beside a sick person signalled a death. He had to agree with Flyte: his medicine had to be very strong.

Please, Granny, please let it work, Reuben begged her. Help me now. It must work!

It *was* like magic. It was like the very best magic. Within hours, the redness and swelling subsided. Baggs's fever departed, leaving him weak but coherent. Later that day, he sat up and called for ale and more tobacco for his pipe.

'Oh! Baggs! It worked. I'm so glad you are well again!' Reuben couldn't suppress a grin, but Baggs didn't smile back.

'Pass me a light, there, Reuben,' said Baggs, wincing as he searched for his tobacco pouch. 'I am better. Didn't I always tell you Doctor Flyte was a great doctor?'

'So,' Flyte said, 'you cheated that magpie, Baggs – his

warning came to nowt. We won't have to leave you here to rot away.'

'I'll be well enough to travel,' said Baggs. 'My face hurts, but you won't need to leave me.' Baggs tried to speak lightly, but it was obvious he had guessed what Flyte had been planning.

'Come here, Reuben!' Flyte said.

Outside, he grabbed Reuben and pushed him up against the cottage wall, his hand to his throat. He thrust his lopsided face up close to him.

'You saved him! You did that!' he hissed, squeezing Reuben's windpipe. 'You and your witchcraft, your spells and your curses!'

'But you said I could try!' cried Reuben, struggling. 'Didn't you want me to?'

Flyte ignored him. 'You've inherited her skills,' he said, darkly. 'I was right. Your root spell had better work, boy, or you'll be in trouble. Understand?'

Reuben nodded vigorously. 'Yes. Yes!'

'Good. Now, before we leave we must collect some real toads for our show. Go bring back five big fat chaps, as warty and evil-looking as you can find!'

Reuben ran down to the river.

Flyte would never expect him to disappear right now. He could go. He could run through the trees and be free! But he needed Shadow.

He flung himself down beside the water and waited

for her. She always appeared when he was alone. He called for her, whistling low and enticingly, but this time, the dog was nowhere to be seen.

'Shadow! Shadow! Where are you? Why aren't you here now we're free to go. Shadow? Shadow, where are you?'

The wagon rumbled along between the straggly hedges towards town. Above them the clouds were heavy, grey and ominous, any hint of spring there might have been had suddenly vanished.

Flyte was in a frighteningly bouncy mood. He reeked of vinegar, having meticulously cleaned his jacket with the stuff. He wore his top hat tipped right on the back of his head; his oily curls tossed in the breeze. He whistled gently as he flicked the reins.

Reuben sat hunched on the bench seat, staring down miserably at a new hole in his ragged trousers.

'Cheer up, little Reuben,' said Flyte, slapping his thigh. 'This is going to be a wonderful day. Aren't you excited at the prospect of performing in front of a crowd? You're going to make my fortune – Toad Eater.'

'I don't think I can do it,' whispered Reuben. 'I'll shake too much. I'll get it wrong. I'll spit it out. Please don't make me.'

Flyte pulled abruptly on the reins, making poor Nellie stumble and snort. The wagon creaked to a standstill.

Flyte turned slowly to face Reuben. Reuben tried to focus on the black spikes of the bare tree branches against the grey sky behind Flyte's head, but he had to meet Flyte's awful eyes.

He began to tremble.

'Reuben. Reuben.' Flyte tweaked at the boy's jacket, smoothed down his shirt, retied the leather strings that laced it down the front. He pushed back Reuben's shoulders; rearranging him, as if the boy was some sort of *thing*. Reuben felt totally powerless as Flyte's long, strong fingers pushed and prodded. He sat immobile and useless.

'You will do it,' Flyte said. 'When I tell you to eat toads, you will. The way we've practised. You will.'

Reuben hung his head.

Baggs chortled. 'And if you don't behave at the fair, I'll make you eat *real* toads, understand?' he said, pinching Reuben. 'Understand?'

'Yes.'

'And don't think we won't,' said Baggs, quietly. ' 'Cos we will.'

Flyte jiggled the reins, urging Nellie to start up again. 'Keep quiet. Do like we've shown you. Everything will run smooth as honey.'

But Reuben was not going to do it. He was not! I'd rather die than cheat, he told himself. And I won't. I won't because I won't be there. I'll run away! Be gone.

First chance. Shadow or no Shadow. This time, I'm running!

They passed along a row of sweet chestnut trees and came to a small hamlet, just three or four cottages gathered around a well. The ground was very muddy and big stones in the road meant they had to trundle slowly past the buildings. At the last cottage, an old man waved them over. He had a small table set up outside his home on which wizened apples were piled together with large leather containers of drink.

'Delicious mead!' he called to them. 'One penny a mug. Come and have a drink!'

'Good idea. We've had no decent drink for days. We will, sir,' said Flyte, stopping the wagon. He got down and bought some mead for himself and for Baggs. While they were drinking, the old man's young daughter came out, carrying a baby. She waved the baby's arm at them.

'Look, little one – visitors,' she said. She smiled at Reuben and offered him a drink too.

'No need for you to pay, little lad,' she said, smiling and holding a mug up to him. 'You have a sip for free.' Her smile was so sweet and she looked so soft and plump, like a fat robin, Reuben wanted to press himself into her, feel her put her arms around him, like she had them round her baby. Something crumbled inside him and he suddenly jumped down from the wagon and ran to her and threw himself at her.

'Oh, please, please!' he said, words gushing out without him stopping to think what he'd say; without a care for Flyte and Baggs watching him. 'Please help me! They've kidnapped me. They're making me go with them and I don't want to. Please! I want to get away. I hate them!' He was on his knees now, his hands snatching at her apron, wrapping themselves in the folds of her skirt. She smelled deliciously of bread and babies and milk. Female things. 'I don't want to eat toads and tell people lies, that's what they'll make me do! Please help me.'

The young woman put her hand on Reuben's head and stroked his hair gently. Reuben felt her touch as keenly as if he'd never been touched before.

'There, there,' she said. 'What's all this, then? There, there.'

Tears welled up at the sound of her kindly voice. She was going to help! Then, just as suddenly as his hope had risen, it died. She was talking to him in a gentle way, but absent-mindedly – the way she spoke to her baby and she was still cooing at the infant while she stroked Reuben. He let go of her skirt. It was no good. It was useless. He'd never escape the Doctor.

Flyte caught hold of him and lifted him to his feet, shaking him like a rug.

'Shut up! Shut up!'

Reuben struggled. 'No! Please! Oh, believe me, mistress!' He tried one more time to convince her and flung himself back at her. 'I don't want to be with them at all! I don't belong to them!'

The old man and his daughter looked at each other in bemusement.

'I've never heard the like,' said the woman, cuddling her baby, and kissing his plump cheek. 'Have you, pet?'

'Please!' Reuben wept.

'What does he mean?' the old man asked, rubbing at his eyes.

'Do you really make the poor lad eat toads?' asked the girl.

'The boy's such a little actor,' Flyte explained, getting hold of Reuben's jacket again. 'He does enjoy the dramatics. We've been teaching him Shakespeare, me and Baggs.'

'That's right,' agreed Baggs.

'No, no, it's not true,' cried Reuben. 'I'm not. I just want my grandmother. Oh, Granny! Granny! I want to go home! They're nothing to me, these two . . .'

The old man was weighing the coins in his hand. He seemed to be considering what Reuben said – *he* at least seemed to believe him, but he was too old, what could he possibly do? It was hopeless.

'Is the boy ill?' asked the old man. 'Why should he take on so?'

'No, no!' sobbed Reuben. 'I'm not! I just hate them! Can't you see? I hate them!'

'Now, Reuben, dear boy,' said Flyte, in a friendly voice, a mild tone that Reuben had never heard before, 'that's not the way to talk to your *father*!'

What? What had he said?

'*Father?*' Reuben spun round and faced him, his tears ceasing instantly. '*Father?*' The lie, the very idea of such a lie, was so terrible! 'You're not my father. He's dead!'

Surely it was a lie to make the old man believe them? But what a lie! It was an outrage!

'No! No!' said Reuben. 'No.'

The old man's wife hobbled out of the cottage.

'What is going on?' she grumbled. 'I told you not to talk to everyone that comes along here and buys your mead, you old fool,' she scolded her husband. 'Now they're having a family dispute on our doorstep. They'll be leaving the boy behind next and we'll be stuck with feeding him. Get away with you! Go on! Get away!' She flapped her stained apron at them as if they were geese who'd invaded her cabbage patch.

'He is not my father. He's no relation at all. Please, listen, you must believe me,' said Reuben, turning to her. 'I'm nothing to do with them. He's not my father. I tell you he's *not* my father. I'm . . .' He was going to tell them about his grandmother, but the words stuck in his throat. How could he explain to them about Sarah Mearbeck being hanged as a witch?

'You see,' Flyte butted in, gently laying his hand on

Reuben, 'he's lost for words. You must stop this foolishness, Reuben. The good people are losing their patience. Of course he's my son,' he added, turning to the old couple and their daughter. 'If it matters at all to you, which it don't, I could prove it. I don't want to waste your time, but . . .'

'Go on then,' said the daughter. 'How can you prove it? Could I prove little Horace here was really my Dan's son?'

Flyte smiled kindly at her. 'You don't need any proof, I'm sure. But it just so happens that I *can* prove he's my son . . .'

'We don't care,' said the old woman. 'Have you paid for that drink?'

'Oh, Mother, let's just see,' said the young woman. 'I'd like to know for sure he belongs with them. He's so sweet, and you do hear about young gentlemen and such being kidnapped.'

'Good folk, let me explain. It's simply a matter of nature . . .' said Flyte, smiling. 'We share the same birthmark.'

Reuben clutched at his neck where his red birthmark was.

'Oh, a birthmark,' the young woman said to her baby. 'You don't have one of those, do you, pet?'

Flyte grabbed Reuben again, ripped back his jacket and shirt and exposed his pale skin.

At the base of Reuben's neck, just where the collarbone joined and made a little hollow, was the red mark like a splattered strawberry, or a splash of blood.

'Oh, well, will you look at that!' said the old man. 'And what are you saying? You've got one the same, have you?'

Flyte peeled back his jacket and shirt and revealed his own bony chest and neck. An identical red splotch showed on his skin.

'Proof,' he said.

'Proof,' agreed the old man, nodding. 'Poor boy, is he soft in the head, then?'

'Just wicked,' said Flyte. 'Intent on mischief. I'll beat it out of him.'

'No! No!' shrieked Reuben. 'It's false. A trick! He is no relation! I swear!'

Baggs took hold of Reuben roughly and pushed him back towards the wagon. 'Little fool!' he spat at him. 'Shut up, you idiot! Ow! Don't struggle! My face!'

Reuben knew he was defeated. Baggs propelled him back up onto the wagon and pushed him onto his seat. Reuben's legs buckled beneath him and he flopped down like a rag doll.

It wasn't true. It couldn't be true. Not Flyte! My father's dead, that's what Granny told me. Reuben's mind raced, looking backwards – images, words, scenes – trying to remember what else his grandmother had told him.

Trying to recall if there were any clues he'd missed. If there was any possibility that this was the truth.

'*I want him. He's mine.*' That's what Flyte had said at The Longford Arms.

Then perhaps he'd wanted him for this reason and not only for his knowledge of potions. Perhaps it was true.

Baggs and Flyte took their places on either side of him, said their farewells and thanks to the old couple and their daughter, and minutes later they were trotting down the lane and out of the hamlet.

At last Flyte said: 'Your grandmother told you your parents died?'

'Yes,' whispered Reuben. 'First my mother, then my father.'

'It wasn't so. Your mother died, but not your father, not me. I went to the wars, doing my duty for the country. Left you with Mother Margaret, in the village. When I got back, you'd gone. *She'd* taken you. Sarah Mearbeck stole you. It took me a long time to trace you. She should've been punished but I was too late – she'd been hanged. The birthmark proves it – you're my son. My property. Mine to do with as I chose.'

Reuben felt so sick he could barely speak. 'I don't believe you. It's not true,' he whispered. His insides seemed to twist and churn and he could hardly get his breath. Where the right side of his body touched Flyte's, the flesh burned. His *father*! No. No. No! But the matching birthmarks? What could that mean?

'Baggs was with Mother Margaret too,' went on Flyte. 'Remember, Baggs? Remember Mother Margaret and her bags?'

Baggs shuddered. 'I remember her.' Baggs rubbed his ears, thinking. 'I remember her place sometimes, before you took me out. I might even remember–' He stopped abruptly as if thinking better of what he was going to say.

'What?' snapped Flyte.

'I thought, well, I thought I remembered a baby with this red thing on its neck, like what Reuben's got. We used to say it was a witch had touched him. And I remember this woman giving us all a green drink . . . and looking for a babe . . . But maybe I don't remember that,' he added, looking up and meeting Flyte's stormy eyes. 'Maybe I'm confused.'

'You are. When I went to get Reuben, my *son*, from that place, and found that he'd gone, I took you, Baggs instead, out of the goodness of my heart.'

'Why didn't you tell me this before?' whispered Reuben.

'Savin' it,' said Flyte. 'Bigger stick to beat you with!'

Reuben tried to speak, but no words came.

'So you just wanted Reuben?' said Baggs. 'Not me, not especially?'

'That's right, I wanted Reuben,' said Flyte. 'What do you say to that, Reuben?'

'Nothing,' said Reuben.

'No, nothing,' agreed Flyte. 'You *know* it's the truth. You feel it in your bones. My *son*. Now you know, there's no escape, no reason to escape. You're with me, where you belong . . .'

21
The Angry Toad

The fair was held in a small town – nothing as grand as Longford, but larger than Willsbridge. There were rows of fine houses boasting real glass windows that flashed in the weak sunlight, coffee houses sending aromatic scents wafting out onto the street, pie shops and pastry shops and a throng of people and animals in the street.

Reuben saw it, but none of it registered.

Flyte is not my father! Granny would never lie to me. I believe what she told me. I love her. She was my real granny, she told me the truth. My father's dead.

The food stalls, tooth-pullers, jugglers and their performing dogs had set up in the field behind the church, but they were beginning to pack up – the fair was almost over and the punters were ready for something new to distract them before the dancing began at dusk. They turned to the newcomers with delight, waving and cheering.

Flyte responded: 'Flyte's Fabulous Formula! The Elixir of the Gods!' Words rolled and slipped from his lips like syrup from a pot. 'Whatever your ill, I can mend you! Fabulous Doctor Flyte is here! Come and see my medicines. Come and see my magical toad.'

They stopped the wagon as soon as they could, not far from the gateway. Baggs stuck a nosebag over Nellie's head before quickly nipping back into the darkness of the wagon's interior where Reuben stood, leaning against the side, thinking, watching.

'Got to hide meself,' Baggs said, indicating his bandaged head. 'Don't look good if Flyte can't mend me, do it?'

'He can't mend anything,' muttered Reuben. 'He's a quack.'

'I should hit you for that!' Baggs sneered, waving a fist at him. 'Ow, me head! It hurts to move about, you scumbag! It's your fault!'

'Oh, hush your nonsense,' said Reuben, wearily. 'Why do you defend him? You–'

'Hurry up!' urged Flyte. 'Damn it, that sour mead's rotting my guts,' he added, leaning over and rubbing his belly. 'Damn that old man's eyes. Now, listen Reuben, listen good. Doctor Brittlebank lives here. The potion you made is for him. I'll tell you as soon as he appears and we'll give it to him. Yes sir! Go on, then. The curtains!' Reuben quickly undid the curtains and folded out the platform at the back of the wagon, making a stage for Doctor Flyte's performance.

Flyte climbed up beside him, muttering under his breath: 'Hell's teeth and buckets of blood, I'm done for. That old man's mead was dog's piss.' But when he faced the people who were beginning to shuffle up to watch, he smiled encouragingly.

'Welcome, everyone!' he yelled. 'Welcome! Get out your money! Let's hear the clink of your coins.' Then an aside to Reuben: 'Reuben, mind you don't get the bottles mixed up,' he hissed. 'Oh, I pray Brittlebank comes! Oh, Brittlebank, Brittlebank, you stuck-up, yellow-livered, fancy-nancy – you'll be pushing up the daisies by nightfall. We'll rot your insides and make your skin boil and fester . . . Toes drop off. Skin go black . . . That's right, madam, I did say toads. I did say Miraculous Medicine!' To Reuben he hissed: 'Keep his bottle on one side, d'you hear? Don't forget. D'you hear?'

Reuben nodded.

By now a good crowd had gathered around the wagon.

'Come on sir, come closer! Look what I've got here. Wonderful potions! Everything for your ailments. All manner of potions. Come on, sir, ladies, girls and boys, come and see!'

Reuben cast a quick glance at the tiny bottle he was supposed to have poisoned. Just coloured water, it was more useless than all the other bottles of the formula and *they* were useless. It only had his pretend curse on it. What could that possibly do?

Perhaps Brittlebank won't turn up today. Oh, I hope he doesn't! Reuben had not gone as far as imagining what would happen if Brittlebank *did* arrive and *did* take the potion and didn't get ill – *that* was too terrible to think of.

He suddenly thought of Shadow. He hadn't seen the dog for two days. Where was she? Why hadn't she followed them? This is the worst day, he thought. The worst day since Granny died. And now I've got to go out in front of all those people. Shadow, please don't abandon me . . .

'Let me delight you with my Fantastic Formula,' Flyte cried. 'I'm no common piss prophet, examining your pee . . . Urine?' Flyte produced a glass bottle containing yellow liquid. 'Whose urine is this?' The crowd laughed as Flyte dipped his finger into the liquid and licked it. 'Does it taste sugary?' He made a surprised and delighted expression. The crowd laughed and squealed. Flyte peered at it again, swilling the stuff round and round. 'Is it black? Do things swim in it? Ugh! No, no!' He put the pot down with a thump. 'I'm not a mere piss prophet. I'm not a faith healer, neither. Nor a quack or a charlatan. I'm a true devotee of Hippocrates. A man of letters! Have I degrees? I've twenty! More,' he cried. 'I've studied in Florence, Dublin and Vienna. I'm a learned man. Science has taught me the ways of the Bile, the Blood, the Choler and the Melancholy. Which one is it that dominates and does you ill? My formula will balance the imbalance and cure you. Yes!' He slapped his thigh. 'We'll cure the cramp, the stitch, the squirt, the itch, the gout, the stone, the pox, the mulligrubs, the bony scrubs and all Pandora's box!'

The crowd laughed and cheered.

'Good citizens, you might ask me why I'm never ill? I'm sure you must wonder at my fortitude in the face of the multitude of fevers I come across in my line of work. I, a man cast down by melancholy . . .' Flyte quickly put on a melancholic expression. 'It is because not only do I take a daily dose of my Fantastic Formula–' he grinned '– but I have something which keeps me from harm, with which to tantalise you today. The *toadstone*.'

'What's that?' a voice from the crowd asked.

'Never heard of it!' shouted another.

'Poor, ignorant souls,' said Flyte, sorrowfully. ' 'Tis the jewel to be found in the head of Bufo bufo – which is the *toad* to you gentle folk. It is the secret stone found in the mysterious, magical toad. Here–' Flyte took the small leather pouch from round his neck '– is a genuine, authentic toadstone. Perhaps you've hard it called Bufonites, or Krottenstein, you may know it simply as the Borax. I call it *The Jewel* because that's what it is, though it's brown and has no sparkle. I myself witnessed its removal from a brown toad, the size of a small dog. It is my most precious possession and I always wear it, here.' He patted his chest. 'It has saved me from the pox, encrustations of the liver, blood clottages, heart seizure and even murder!'

The crowd gasped, turning to each other in wonder.

'Yes, *murder*. One dark night, deep in the narrow, evil streets of London, a vagabond crept up on me. His intentions? To do me ill! Before he pounced, I felt a burning in my chest, just where the toadstone lies, nestling in its leather bed. I put my hand up to it and at that moment, the vagabond – the would-be murderer – struck with his knife . . . Like so!' Flyte jabbed the air with an invisible knife, making the onlookers jump back in alarm. 'But I caught it!' This he did also, with much pulling and tussling with his invisible assailant. 'Inches away from my chest. If the stone hadn't burned and warned me, I'd be a dead man by now. But the dead man, ladies and gentlemen, was my attacker!'

A ripple of applause ran through the crowd.

'On other occasions I have reduced fevers, saved injured limbs and caused the cessation of bleeding – just with my stone. The toadstone is a truly fabulous phenomenon. So wonderful—' his voice rose, then softened, lingering on the words, tantalising his listeners '— so magical, that the toad wants it back!'

The audience murmured and whispered.

'Watch!' Flyte held up his palm, demanding their silent attention. 'Let me show you the enormous and extraordinary power of the toadstone. So glorious is the stone's power that when a toad sees it, it is consumed with envy and leaps towards it, desperate to repossess it!'

Flyte stood a small, square table on the platform then quickly placed a rounded object, shaped like a pudding, on it. A white cloth covered it from view.

The crowd craned their necks to see.

'Behold! The terrible, awesome Toad!' Flyte whisked off the cloth, revealing a large glass dome, beneath which sat a squat, brown toad.

Behind the curtain, Baggs had been teasing the poor creature, poking it with sticks, dangling it by its back legs, and generally driving it wild. The toad was as bad-tempered as a toad could be.

'Watch, ladies and gentlemen! Watch!' Flyte held the toadstone up. 'Now, feast your peepers on this!' He gently lifted up the glass cover and thrust the toadstone at the toad.

It couldn't have worked better. It was exactly as Flyte had described. The toad reared up on its hind legs in an unnatural way and lunged towards the toadstone, its wide mouth gaping hungrily, as though it was trying to grab the stone back.

'Ahh!' the audience fell backwards in amazement and horror.

'No,' murmured Reuben, involuntarily. It was just the same behaviour the toad had shown the day Old John died. It was nothing to do with toadstones! It couldn't be! It was just the creature's display of anger and frustration.

'See how jealous it is!' Flyte was saying, quickly slipping the glass back over the animal. 'He wants it back! He wants it for himself, but he can't have it. It's mine . . . Ah! What?' Flyte cupped a hand to his ear, pretending to hear voices of doubt in the crowd. 'You distrust me? You don't believe in my toadstones or my Fantastic Formula? You want to see them at work on a human being? Well, let me introduce you to–' he flung back the curtain, 'REUBEN!'

Reuben stared at the wagon floor, aware of the sea of searching, inquisitive, hungry faces turned towards him. He twisted his hands into the fabric of his trousers, unable to move.

'*Reuben!*' Flyte's voice was harder and sharper the second time.

Reuben looked up at his master. There was no question that he would step forward and show the audience just what Flyte wanted them to see, his legs, though, wouldn't work. His feet, he was sure, were nailed to the floor. He kept looking into Flyte's eyes. If eyes could burn, if eyes were tinders, ready to flare, then so were Flyte's eyes.

'Reuben? Step forward, boy.'

The audience couldn't see the suspicion of violence, the menace of threat in his voice and eyes as he glared at Reuben. Flyte turned back to the crowd, anxious not to lose them. 'This lad – this small, simple lad – is going to show you just how potent and fantastic my medicine is – aren't you, Reuben?'

Reuben glanced back at Baggs.

'Go on!' hissed Baggs, grinning and licking his lips. 'Yummy yum! Juicy toad!' he whispered.

Reuben stepped forward. His heart hung suspended in his chest, painful and full. Oh, somebody, save me! he begged. But no one was there to hear him.

Flyte touched him on the shoulder and Reuben shuddered at the feel of his fingers on him.

'This boy trusts me. He trusts my elixir. So entirely does he trust us both, that I am going to perform an extraordinary and dangerous experiment on him. Stand back, everyone. Stand back!'

The crowd obediently moved a pace back, stepping on toes and jostling each other nervously.

Flyte lifted the toad out from under the cover and held it, cupped, in his hand.

Some of the women crossed themselves. Toads were witches' mediums. Toads were poisonous and in league with the Devil. Toads lived in dark, damp cellars and holes, and anything that did so must surely be hiding for a good reason.

'As you good people know,' said Flyte, 'toads are venomous. Why, even to lick your fingers after touching a toad can be fatal. But this boy – this small, thin boy of mine – will show amazing strength and courage and he will *eat* this toad. Yes, I did say *eat*. He will eat this poisonous creature, right now, before your very eyes, and when the poison has begun to take action – which won't be long, ladies, not long – then I will administer my amazing tonic, my Fabulous Formula, and you will see a remarkable, immediate and full recovery!'

'It's dangerous!' said a man in the audience. 'Does he know what he's doing?'

'Me or the boy?' laughed Flyte. He held out the toad to the man who'd spoken. 'Touch the beast, sir,' he suggested. 'Touch his skin and taste his evil exuberances.'

'Not me! I wouldn't!'

One young man, egged on by his girl, dared to touch the dry skin of the toad, then tentatively licked his finger. 'Agh!' He spat on the ground. 'It's foul!'

The crowd murmured darkly.

'Will I die, sir?' croaked the youth, spitting violently.

'Quick, take a sip of my remedy,' Flyte said, uncorking a bottle, pouring out a spoonful and handing it to the lad. 'I won't charge you for that, sir – you were brave, sir.'

The youth gulped the liquid and found himself still alive.

'That's a good taste,' he muttered. 'That must be fine stuff. I'll buy some.'

'Later, young sir, later. Now, Reuben, come!'

Reuben could not control his shakes. He knew he was

pale, his head felt as if all the blood had drained away to his toes. The audience was impressed; the boy was scared. The sea of wide-eyed faces focused on him with hideous anticipation.

What if it went wrong? What if the boy couldn't do it? Or he died?

The toad sat hunched on Flyte's palm, gulping, blinking. Silly, senseless toad, thought Reuben.

'Ready?'

Flyte set the creature down on the table and swiftly lay a dark cloth over it. 'I shall spare you the blood, ladies. I don't want you to see it squirm and dance!'

He took up a wooden mallet and stood, poised.

'Go on!' someone roared.

THWACK! The mallet cracked against the table with a sound like a ripe orange exploding.

The crowd leaped as one. Some cried out. One woman screamed.

'No matter, it's done,' said Flyte, half turning his face to them, grinning wickedly. He produced a long, sharp knife from a shelf alongside and quickly sliced off the toad's hind leg, letting it dangle, dripping, from his hand. The leg seemed to live on, twitching as it hung there.

'No, you can't make him do that!' cried a woman in the audience. 'Don't let him eat it!'

'The poor boy!'

There was a loud whisper from the back of the wagon: 'Go on, Reuben, speak!'

Reuben said weakly, 'It's a strong medicine. I shall not suffer.'

He opened his mouth.

Flyte held up the toad. There was a moment where Reuben seemed to change his mind, put up his hand as a barrier to prevent Flyte from putting the leg into his mouth, and behind this temporary shield, Flyte popped the dough leg into Reuben's open mouth. The sleight of hand was so quick that nobody noticed it. Even Reuben, for one terrible moment, thought he was biting down on the real thing.

Reuben closed his eyes and chewed.

'Ah, ooh, ugh!' cried the horrified audience.

'Poor boy!'

'He'll die!'

'It tastes rotten,' said the young man who'd licked it. 'I can vouch for that!'

They watched, spellbound, following every fleeting expression that crossed Reuben's face. First distaste and horror, then, as he crunched loudly, and his eyes grew rounder and rounder . . . disgust and FEAR!

Suddenly Reuben began to twitch. First his legs, then his arms, and then his head. He jerked and jigged like a puppet. He began to groan. Low moans and wails flew from his pale lips. He sank to the floor, quivering. 'Help me!' he cried. 'I'm poisoned.'

The crowd pressed closer, murmuring and crying:

'Will he die?'

'Murderer!'

'Give him help!'

Now Reuben was foaming at the mouth. Lumps of a strange, speckled grey matter were spilling from his lips. His eyes were rolling backwards in his head. He writhed, kicking and spinning round on the floor.

'Do something for him! Make him better!'

'Please don't panic,' said Flyte, calmly. 'Everything is under control. One drop of my elixir will bring him back to health.'

Standing in full view of the crowd, he slowly unstoppered a bottle of Flyte's Fantastic Formula and spooned it into Reuben's open mouth.

Nothing happened. Reuben lay like a dead thing. The audience went very still. One voice cried out:

'You did it too late, you've killed him!'

22
Flyte's Last Performance

'No, look! He's moving!'

'The poor little chap!'

'Is he all right?'

Reuben gradually started to move, testing his limbs and opening his eyes. He put out his hand for more formula, was given some, then slowly, slowly, sat himself up and looked around at the crowd as if he'd never seen them before, as if he'd no idea where he was, or what had happened.

'What happened? Did I fall over? I'm well,' he said in a small voice. 'I've never felt so well.' He stood up slowly. 'I feel wonderful!'

The audience went wild. They cheered and called and shouted. They stamped their feet and waved their hats in the air. Then, as the same idea occurred to them all at exactly the same moment, they surged forward simultaneously, eager to buy Flyte's Fantastic Formula or Flyte's Fantastic Toadstones.

A woman grabbed Reuben's arm. 'Are you really better? Did that medicine make you well?'

Reuben hesitated.

'I didn't–' he began, when an arm shot out through

the curtains and Baggs squeezed him viciously.

'It did, ma'am,' Baggs muttered, keeping half hidden. 'It's very good. And he wears his toadstone, too, to keep him safe.'

'Will it help my little Henry, d'you think?' She uncovered a bundle in her arms. The baby was grey-skinned, thin; his brown eyes like two big conkers in his peaked, pale face.

'Oh, poor mite,' said Reuben.

'Of course it will cure him!' said Flyte. 'Buy a bottle and see how his Humours disappear and how sprightly he'll become. It's the Bile, madam, the Bile that does it. Buy a toadstone too, keep the evil spirits away and–'

'Stop!' A loud, authoritative voice erupted above the hubbub, and everyone fell silent. 'Stop!'

A small, plump man – the owner of the surprisingly big booming voice – was pushing his way forward through the crowd.

'Stop! The man's a charlatan! He's a quack and a fraud! A jackdaw in peacock's feathers! Don't buy that rubbish!' he bawled. 'Don't you dare give him your money! Stop! Stop, I say!'

Flyte had gone as still as a statue. He was staring at the man as if he were the Devil himself. Hatred gleamed in his dark eyes.

'It's him,' he hissed quietly over his shoulder. '*Brittlebank*.'

Reuben shivered. This was Brittlebank, the man he was to poison and curse but he didn't look bad, he looked kind . . .

The little man was a well-dressed gentleman. He carried a walking stick, his jacket was embroidered and his hat boasted a long feather plume. He elbowed everyone out of the way and the villagers – their money still clenched in their fists – fell back, waiting and watching. Several of them took off their hats and muttered greetings to him.

'Well, Flyte, I didn't think you'd dare show your ugly face here again,' growled Brittlebank. 'Not after last time. Still peddling coloured water? Still selling useless stones?'

Flyte glowered down at him.

'It's *Doctor* Flyte,' he said.

'And it's *Doctor* Brittlebank,' mimicked the man, adjusting his gold spectacles, 'expect that I happen to be a qualified man of science. Happen to have truthfully studied in Florence and London. I am a *real* doctor and you are nothing but a quack!'

'He cured the boy!' someone said.

'We saw it with our own eyes.'

'He's got toadstones.'

'His formula works like magic.'

'Aye, I bet it does,' said Doctor Brittlebank. 'With the help of that lying little scoundrel acting for him. I warned you last time you came here, Flyte; if you set foot here again, I'd run you out of the town like a beggar. No more swindling and lying. I will not see my neighbours and patients wasting their hard-earned money on this rubbish! Get out of here or there'll be trouble for you.'

Reuben coloured with shame. He dragged the curtain around him. I'm innocent, I'm innocent; he willed the doctor to hear his thoughts.

'Oh, trouble is it?' said Flyte, idly flicking a handkerchief through the air. 'And what trouble are you thinking of?'

'I'll run you out of town myself,' roared the doctor, shaking his fist, 'and your dirty little accomplice too.'

'If my formula is so useless,' said Flyte, calmly, 'will you try it? Will you take some now, in front of all these people and then say it's no good?'

'Of course I will!' said Doctor Brittlebank. 'I'll drink ten bottles and not be any better or worse, since it's nothing but a few herbs and spices in water and you're nothing but a cheap, lying imposter!'

'Is that right?' said Flyte slowly. 'Well, well. Reuben, be so good as to pass me *the* bottle, please.'

Reuben couldn't do it. He couldn't move.

'*Reuben?*' Flyte's voice was heavy with menace.

Reuben stepped back and knocked into Baggs.

'Do it,' Baggs hissed, so close his breath was hot on his neck.

With a thundering heart and trembling fingers,

Reuben took the special bottle from its hiding place. It'll be all right, he reminded himself. There's nothing really special about it at all, it's worthless – herbs and water, just like the real doctor said.

'Thank you, Reuben,' said Flyte, grinning and snatching the bottle from him. 'Here you are then, good sir, take a sip of this!'

As the bottle was handed from Reuben, to Flyte, and from Flyte to Doctor Brittlebank, the audience followed it closely with their eyes.

Brittlebank uncorked the small bottle and sniffed the contents. 'Salts of ammonia,' he said, 'fennel, rosemary . . . nothing of any value at all! Three pennies! A waste of good money! Pah!'

And he drank the whole thing down in one gulp.

Doctor Brittlebank smacked his lips and stoppered up the bottle. He returned Flyte's confident smile. He turned round to the audience, as if he was about to repeat his words on the uselessness of the tonic. He even opened his mouth, but then it all went horribly wrong.

His expression changed, his eyes bulged, he screamed as if scalded and clutched at his throat, yelling and crying. He spun round, he danced on his toes, yelping and whining like a wounded animal.

'He's dying! Poison!' A woman shouted. 'Our doctor's bewitched!'

The crowd whispered and nudged each other, shuffling about, not knowing what to do.

Reuben dropped to his knees, his hands at his own throat in sympathy.

Oh, those silly things I said! he thought. The way I pressed the thorns into the man-root! I did it! I really did a curse. No, no, he contradicted himself. My potion couldn't work! I didn't do that! I couldn't! Reuben gasped, he could barely breathe, his heart was stopping up his throat, there was a weight, like a heap of earth, heavy on his chest.

Doctor Brittlebank twisted and jumped. 'I've been poisoned! I'm dying! Help me!' He began to stagger backwards and forwards as if pulled back and forth by invisible threads. 'Oh God, it's much worse than I feared, it's much worse! It's burning! It's dissolving my insides! Don't buy that stuff, good people, don't touch his medicine, it'll . . . it'll . . . kill you!'

He slumped to the ground like a sack of grain.

Pandemonium broke out.

Men yelled, women screamed. Some ran to help the doctor, others turned on the potion-sellers. Stones were picked up and hurled at the wagon, along with rude abuse. Children whooped and laughed and skittered around wildly. Skirts twirled, sticks were waved. The ravens lifted from the rubbish pile and rose into the air like a black cloud. Somewhere a dog barked and barked.

While helping hands surrounded the prostrate doctor, the wagon was surrounded by violent ones.

'Murderers! Devils!'

Fists rained down on them, clawing fingers grabbed at them.

Flyte kicked and shouted. Managing to wrench himself from their grasp, he pulled himself into the back of the cart and yanked up the platform. He grabbed Reuben by the collar, hitting him hard round the head as he did so.

'You ass!' he hissed through clenched teeth. 'What did you do?' His face was inches from Reuben's, his spit splattered his cheek. 'I told you! I said it should work in *hours*! Not immediately! Not like that!'

Suddenly the wagon lurched forward.

'Get on, Nellie!' Baggs shouted and Nellie sprang off at a gallop, sending Flyte toppling over and hundreds of tiny glass bottles tumbling from the shelves. Jars, plates, books, papers and powders cascaded down over them.

'God's teeth!' roared Flyte, cracking his head on the corner of the cupboard. 'Take care, Baggs!'

The wagon flew, jolting, swaying, zigzagging – sending the angry crowd spinning off in all directions. It tipped, rolled precariously on two wheels, nearly toppled, then righted itself with a thundering crash, smashing another stall, before gathering speed as Nellie sped off down the lane.

Reuben bumped and rolled. He tried to catch hold of

something, grab anything, to right himself. He clawed his fingers into the upholstery and managed to pull himself halfway up, to stare out through the flapping curtains at the furious crowd, as it got smaller and smaller, retreating into the distance.

In the driving seat, Baggs – a wild, crazy expression on his face, his bandage unravelling around his neck – stood with his feet braced against the sides, cracking the reins against Nellie's back. 'Get up there, Nellie!'

Flyte was rolling back and forth on the floor, tangled in rope, clothes, bottles and crockery. 'Help me, you fool!' The wagon bounced and bumped. 'Give me a hand!'

Reuben didn't move. In two seconds he made up his mind. This was it! His only chance!

He crouched, ready to spring.

As the wagon swerved round the first corner, he jumped.

The speed of the racing wagon threw him out hard against a tangle of bushes and rocks. Dazed and hurt, he got to his feet as quickly as he could and, without looking round, ran for cover, diving into the ditch beside the lane, narrowly missing hitting the milestone, wedged into the grass.

Stonebridge.

The milestone said Stonebridge . . . why did that suddenly seem important? He shook his head. Was he losing his mind? Where had he heard that name? Something to do with the old days . . . his grandmother . . .

He didn't want to think. He hadn't *time* to think. He scrambled under low branches, slithered between bushes and trees and worked his way further and further into the woods, finally squeezing himself between two rounded boulders where he sat, gulping, just like a toad.

He stayed as still as he could, listening to the silence. No sign of Baggs and Flyte. Nothing, just his breath whistling through his chest and the blood swooshing through his head.

Stonebridge. Of course it meant something to him. Stonebridge was where his grandmother had told him to go! Where her cousin lived. He thumped his forehead against the rock until it hurt.

Now I can never come back! They'll recognise me. The only place I wanted to come to and I've spoiled it!

And Brittlebank? The doctor? Was he dead? Did I really make a magic potion by mistake?

He squeezed himself into the smallest size possible; so miserable, all he could do was huddle there, mouth hanging open, eyes to the sky, and let rip a soundless howl. I can't bear it! I can't! Am I to be pushed out of my home, my life, like a flea-bitten cat, a rat, a tick, nobody – other than Flyte – wanting me? Where can I go? What can I do? I'll never go back to Flyte. He's not my father. I don't believe it, whatever he says, it isn't true. Oh, Granny, what am I going to do?

For hours he hardly moved.

His mind wandered.

He found himself thinking back to his other life, the happy life with his grandmother in Pleck Cottage. He tried to remember what she'd ever said about his parents, desperate to disprove Flyte's story. Why would his grandmother lie? She would never lie. Or might she just not have told him the whole truth?

The sky darkened and the cold crept around him; invisible fingers of bitterness that wrapped round his bones and made them ache. His toes and fingertips lost all sense of feeling. Hunger squeezed his stomach. He knew he'd have to move – or die there.

Then I'll stay, he decided. If I move on, it'll have to be moving on in the wrong direction, and on again, and again, and I can't do that. It's unjust! It's not right. I'd rather stay here and die then. I don't care. I don't care any more!

A tiny sound caught his attention.

Someone was near. Someone was there in the woods, creeping towards him. Flyte! It had to be – or Baggs! They mustn't find him. Surely they wouldn't, not in this gloomy blue twilight. Surely he was almost invisible in his rocky hideout. He stared out at the tangle of brambles, bushes and tree trunks. All around him it seemed the trees were creeping closer, the sky pressing down with the approaching night.

Twigs snapped and leaves rustled rhythmically as if whoever it was, moving so relentlessly towards him, was beating back the foliage with a stick. Swish! Swish! Soon they were so close he could hear their breathing . . . A foul, wet, animal smell filled his nostrils . . .

'Shadow!'

The dog's long snout burst through the greenery beside him, her wagging tail slashing the leaves, *swish, swish.* Reuben squeezed out from his hideout and wrapped his arms around her, felt the dog's whiskers brushing his cheeks, her tongue busy on his hands.

'Oh, Shadow, how did you find me? Where've you been? How did you get here?' The dog licked his face in answer and Reuben pushed her away. 'You stink. Smelly creature.' Shadow wagged her tail. 'Shadow, you always come back, don't you?'

Shadow cocked her head on one side, ears up, tail waving.

'What shall we do? Where to go? Help me.'

Shadow immediately got up and trotted off, heading back towards Stonebridge, turning to check Reuben was following.

'No, Shadow, no, we mustn't. Not that way!'

Shadow stopped, ears pricked and whined.

'They'll hang me for murder,' he told the dog. 'Don't you know that?'

Still the dog turned towards Stonebridge, her black nose wrinkling as she lifted it slighty to sniff the air.

'Can't you hear me?' Reuben hissed, exasperated. 'Don't you know what I'm saying? We can't go that way. Nor that,' he added, looking in the direction the wagon had taken. 'Come, Shadow, we'll have to go this way.'

He patted his thigh but the dog wouldn't come.

'Shadow!' Reuben had some twine in his pocket. He made a slip-knot with it. 'Sorry, Shadow. But we must go the other way, we must.'

Shadow ducked her head, resisting the makeshift leash that Reuben tried to slip around her neck; she even growled softly. 'I know. I'm sorry. But I can't do it alone. I need you, and you don't understand, I know. But this is the right way.'

Together they moved quietly and slowly back onto the lane. Reuben was alert to every sound but there was nothing. Nothing to see, either, in the murky twilight.

'We'll just walk, and walk,' he whispered to Shadow. 'I remember a crossroads, and some buildings back that way. We could branch off there and hide for the night. What d'you think? And we'll find somewhere in the end. Where no one knows us. I'll get work in the fields, and if I can't, well, we'll eat berries and herbs and we'll live in a cave together.'

Reuben pulled up his jacket collar tightly round his neck; if only he had his cloak.

'That doctor will be all right,' he told Shadow. 'He must be. I didn't do anything to him because I can't, can I, Shadow? I'm no more a witch than Granny was. We don't believe in witchcraft, do we? Not the Devil, not dolls made of roots that carry curses, none of it. Oh, why did I let Flyte make me do it? Why did I pretend? I wish I never had!'

Reuben tried to ignore the way the greenery on either side rose into weird black phantom shapes and the way the wind whined in the tall trees. He patted the dog's head, glad of the feel of her fur against his hand and of her warmth beside him.

They passed cottages, where lighted candles flickered at the windows. Smoke drifted from their chimneys and filled the air with a comforting, woody scent. Reuben pictured the people snug inside in the warmth. One day, he thought, I'll have that again. One day.

'Good girl. Splendid dog. We'll be good together. Good girl . . .'

Suddenly, Shadow stopped, her feet firmly bedded into the ground. She barked sharply. Immediately alert, Reuben sidestepped towards the low wall that ran alongside that stretch of the lane. But he wasn't quick enough. Without warning, two figures leaped out at him, silently landing on him like falling trees, throwing him hard to the ground.

Shadow's rope slipped from Reuben's hand.

'No! Shadow! Come back!'

But the dog had gone, vanishing into the trees like a whisper.

Reuben had no time to register the enormity of Shadow's abandoning him, because Flyte was roaring at him, shaking him like an old mat and Baggs was raining blows at any part of him he could reach.

'You scoundrel! You snake! You tried to trick me! You nearly got me killed! You'll pay for this, you certainly will.' Flyte began walloping him around the head with the flat of his hand until Reuben shook from side to side.

'Ow! Ow! Stop!' He was no match for the bigger, stronger man, so instead, he suddenly dropped to his knees, as if he'd fainted.

Flyte let go in surprise. 'Have I done him too hard?'

It gave Reuben a second's advantage. He launched into the air like a deer, kicking Flyte hard on the knee and slipped past him and past Baggs, and on down the lane.

Reuben ran. He ran like the wind, his tough boots thudding on the hard ground, his arms pumping at his sides. He pushed his chin forward, sucked air greedily into his lungs. The ground sped by beneath him.

But Baggs was right behind. His longer legs covered the distance so much faster, thumping, thumping, the reverberations travelled right up into Reuben's head.

'*No!*' Reuben yelled. 'Leave me! Let me go!'

He ran on, stumbling, leaping tall grasses and stones. 'You won't get me. You can't get me. No, no, no!'

But now Baggs was right behind him, snorting, panting and wheezing like an old horse. Reuben felt a sudden rush as Baggs threw himself at him, flung all his weight at him and brought him crashing down with such force the breath squeezed from his chest like air from a bellows. His head hit the ground, his neck snapped painfully. Stunned, he lay totally still.

'Got you, you pisspot!' Baggs roared, wrenching his arm up behind his back. 'You little squit. Lying witch boy. You're dead!'

23
A Night in the Woods

Reuben lay squashed on the earth with Baggs, like a sack of potatoes, on top of him.

'You've near ruined our lives, maggot!' Baggs panted. 'Near killed me. Near killed the Doctor. You're bad luck. Bad! Wish we'd never found you! He rolled off Reuben, grabbed his arm, twisted it up his back, then used it to haul him to his feet. The pain almost made Reuben faint. 'Now, wait till the Doctor catches up,' Baggs spluttered. 'Then you're for it, Stick. Flyte's in such a frenzy!'

Reuben felt as though his brain was shaken loose and wobbling in his skull. Lights danced in front of his eyes, waves of throbbing pain washed over his scalp. There was a sharper pain above his left eye and he could feel blood trickling down his forehead.

Shadow had gone! That was the worst. Nothing hurt so much as that.

I should never have tied her up. She's not that sort of dog. I should have gone the way she wanted. I betrayed her somehow.

An owl hooted. Baggs chuckled, then replied with a similar cry, and a few moments later Flyte crept out of the shadows and crouched beside them.

'Men on the road,' he whispered. 'Coming this way. Hide.'

They tumbled Reuben through the thorns, leaves and rocks and rolled into a ditch. Baggs clamped his dirty hand over Reuben's mouth, keeping up the pressure on his aching elbow.

'Not a murmur,' hissed Flyte.

It was dark now, not much of a moon, and they were well hidden.

Footsteps approached. A glow from burning sticks and lanterns illuminated four men. Reuben couldn't see their faces but he heard their voices clearly.

'Can't understand where they've gone,' one said. 'Was sure we'd cut them off here, Doctor.'

'They've gone to ground, I shouldn't wonder. It's easy to hide in the scrub and woods.'

Reuben froze. It was Doctor Brittlebank! He craned his neck, trying to see. The doctor wasn't dead!

But I saw him drop! thought Reuben. How was he now alive? Thank God he's alive, but – I'm trapped either way: Flyte or Brittlebank, they'll both do for me!

'We must find them. That quack and his toad-eating boy are for the noose!'

'What'll we do now, Doctor?' said another voice.

'You two go back on the road into Stonebridge, see if there's any marks to show where they left the road . . .' He hesitated. 'No, damn it! It's too dark now. We'd best start again, first thing in the morning. I don't want Flyte getting away a second time. We must apprehend them all!'

The light faded, their footsteps receded and soon all was quiet and dark again.

Flyte let out a low whistle. 'Reuben, Reuben, Reuben,' he said, shaking his head.

'Told you his potion weren't no good,' said Baggs. 'Didn't kill the little Doctor after all. What went wrong with it? Your witchcraft and spells? Did you cheat the good Doctor Flyte? Your father!'

Reuben pursed his lips and shook his head. He didn't understand what had happened to Doctor Brittlebank either, but he was so glad.

'You ragged us, you little bugger!' Baggs slapped him round the back of his head.

'Betrayed by my own son,' said Flyte. He got slowly to his feet, dragging Reuben with him.

'We're near the road here,' said Baggs. 'We could–'

Flyte snatched the tinder box from him and struck a flint to light a candle. 'Here, give us the lantern. Don't get any ideas, Baggs, it don't suit you . . . I make the plans.'

A few moments later the soft glow lit them up. Flyte's face was streaked with dirt. He'd lost his tall hat. His bent beak-like nose looked more bent than ever.

'They'd've found us if they'd looked a wee bit further,'

he muttered. 'We were lucky there. Come on. This way.'

He led them down a narrow track and into the blackness of the woods to the wreckage of their wagon.

When Baggs had been driving them out of Stonebridge, his only thought had been to get away fast and get hidden. He had driven Nellie recklessly, steering the wagon right into the forest, over the uneven ground, over bushes and stones. He'd aimed for a gap that was too small, and now the wagon was tightly wedged between two trees. One of the massive back wheels was crooked, some spokes splintered. Broken pots and plates, overturned pans and boxes, lay strewn around.

'Splendid horsemanship, Baggs,' muttered Flyte as they came into the clearing.

'It was the–'

'Shut it.'

Scowling, Baggs threw Reuben to the ground and tied his hands and legs firmly to a wheel with thin, hard rope. 'No way you're moving,' he said, yanking the knots tight. 'Not this time.'

'It wasn't my fault,' said Reuben.

'No?'

'I mean, maybe Doctor Brittlebank had an antidote,' said Reuben, thinking quickly. 'If you take one soon enough, even the best poison is no good. Honestly.'

Flyte looked dangerous. He was pacing backwards and

forwards, his face was very pale, his dark eyes glowering beneath his thick brows.

'Be silent!'

'But it's true. I didn't cheat you. I just – maybe it wasn't strong enough? Maybe Doctor Brittlebank didn't really drink it?'

Flyte glared at him, disbelief showing in his hooded eyes. 'I saw him!'

'But . . .'

'Quiet.' Flyte gazed round at the broken wagon and scattered mess. 'This is your fault. My own son, turning against me! What a rascal, eh?'

My son. My son. Reuben retched at the words. It was not true!

Baggs began to build a fire. 'I'll get us some grub, Doctor,' he said. 'We'll be fine.'

'I'm not hungry,' said Flyte. 'I told you. I've got cramps from that mead. Guts griping. I need the bushes.' He staggered off. 'Keep an eye on him, Baggs,' he called back over his shoulder. 'I'll deal with him when I get back.'

He disappeared into the darkness.

Reuben closed his eyes. His throbbing head pulsed painfully. Doctor Brittlebank wasn't dead! His insides seemed to melt and go hot. Not dead. He wasn't a murderer. The doctor must have been acting, and by pretending to be ill, he'd prevented anyone else from buying the useless formula.

Reuben looked up as Baggs threw some branches of dry wood onto the fire and a shower of sparks fell around him.

'Baggs!'

'What?'

'Baggs, let me go. Please. What does it matter to you? You hate me, you don't want me around. If you let me go I'll just creep away like a little mouse, you'll never see me again. I'll disappear. Baggs, I saved you, remember? I saved your life. I mended your face.'

Baggs chucked another log on the fire, casting a sideways look at him.

'I did, Baggs. Flyte would've left you to die. I patched you up and–'

'Nah,' said Baggs, shaking his head, then stopping abruptly and grimacing at the pain. 'Ow! It throbs like a drum! Nah, that was Flyte. He'd never leave me die. *He* saved me.'

'How could he save you, Baggs? He doesn't know the first thing about medicine . . .'

'Don't say that! You only know curses and how to give people the evil eye. Terrible potion-making you can do, and weird bad spells with roots. You tried to kill me, Reuben and I know it.' He stared into the dancing flames, feeling the edges of his dirty bandage, prodding the still swollen skin. 'You've got magic powers.'

'Baggs, I haven't, really. I tried to save you.'

'Never.'

'I could have run away when you were so ill and the fever was making you rave and scream, but I didn't. I stayed with you.'

Baggs stared into the flames. 'Flyte stayed with me,' he said, doggedly.

'Flyte? Oh, Baggs! He doesn't care about anyone, don't you see that? And now I fear he plans to kill me . . .'

'Aye, he will,' agreed Baggs and grinned. 'And we'll be better off without you. I never wanted you. Me and the doctor got on fine without you. What'd he want a scrawny boy like you as a son for? There's other lads would've been much better.'

'Please . . .'

But just then, Flyte hobbled back into the circle of firelight. He was doubled up with pain and clutching his stomach.

'Damn squits,' he moaned. 'Brandy! Pass me the brandy.'

Baggs lumbered off to search for the drink amongst the boxes lying on the ground.

'Lucky it weren't broken,' he said, passing over the heavy bottle. 'Here you go.'

Flyte uncorked it with his teeth and took a long swig. 'Baggs, I'm too churned up for anything. The gripes are bad. We can't do it tonight. I'll never find the place I want and–'

'Do what?' asked Baggs.

'Gawd! Do you have any brain at all? Get rid of the boy. We don't want his body found neither,' said Flyte. He took more of his drink. 'There's a mine shaft further in the woods. Lead or tin, some such they used to find here. It's called Cal's Cauldron–'

'Cal's Cauldron?' Baggs repeated, looking up. 'I've heard of it.'

' 'Course you haven't,' snapped Flyte. 'Don't be stupid.'

'Oh, I thought . . .' Baggs chewed his lip.

'We'll drop him down it,' went on Flyte. 'Look like an accident.'

Reuben looked from one to the other. They couldn't do that to him! Nobody could be so cruel, so evil . . .

'You know these woods, then?' asked Baggs.

'Like the back of my hand,' Flyte said, sitting down beside the fire with the brandy bottle in his hands. 'I was born in Stonebridge. I know every nook and cranny of the place.'

'Borned here? You never said!' cried Baggs, indignantly.

'Why should I? What's it to you?'

'Never thought of you being born anywhere,' muttered Baggs, sticking out his bottom lip.

Flyte snorted with laughter. 'Pudding-head.'

They sank into silence. The fire crackled. Flyte swallowed more brandy. Baggs picked anxiously at his bitten nails.

Reuben watched their faces, tinged pink and yellow in the dancing light of the fire. Flyte looked so devilish. The black shadows played over his face, accentuating his asymmetrical features, his pointed chin. Devil man! Beast! Do you really mean to throw me down a hole and leave me to die? I'd rather be killed swiftly with a knife or a blow to the head. Not a slow, lonely death in the dark . . . I could last for days and days. Shadow! Shadow, where are you now?

I don't want to die.

When Granny died I'd have been happy to be hanged too. Glad of it. To go away. Be out of life. What a long time ago that seems! But now I want to live. I want to find our cousin in Stonebridge, tell Doctor Brittlebank the truth. Find Shadow. And I want to have ideas, like Granny said. Want to know why things work or don't work. I want to be a medicine man. I want to make all the little Georges in all the villages of England well again. There's so much I want to and need to do. No time for dying!

Baggs appeared to have been deep in thought too, and suddenly said: 'That Brittlebank – did you know him, Doctor Flyte? I mean, when you lived here, in Stonebridge?'

‘ ’Course I knew him,’ said Flyte, rounding on Baggs, fiercely. ‘I know most people in Stonebridge, though they don’t remember me. I was little Bartholomew Flyte. Not worth noticing. Worth nothing.’

Baggs chewed that over and at last said: ‘Last time we came here, that Brittlebank tried to make out you was a fraud. He said you was a quack. He tried to stop you.’

‘Aye, and I’d come back to be admired and respected!’ snarled Flyte. ‘That’s when I vowed to return and pay him back. For that and all the past injustices he’s meted out to me.’

‘Why didn’t they like you? I mean when you were younger and all?’

‘Baggs, I’ve had just about enough of your questions, you lumpen idiot,’ snapped Flyte. But his anger flared and was gone as he drank more brandy and settled himself more comfortably with his cloak and blanket around him. Words slipped out easily, slurring as they came, as if he couldn’t help himself.

‘There was only me and an old auntie; an old dame, like your granny, Reuben – a dried up old rind, all bone and gristle. She’d had no man to love, that’s a fact. No man’d ever loved her. No titties. Face like thunder. I hated her. I hated her so badly. She was as mean as a crow. Beat me. Made a fool out of me. Had me sleep outside with the stinking dogs. Worked me worse than a horse. She mocked my voice, my looks – made the kids taunt me too 'cos I were an ugly nothin'. They threw stones at me. Brittlebank was the worst. He thought he were so grand since he knew his letters and wore a bit of lace! I hated him for that fancy lace and his books and learning and calling me long names . . . and I hate him now.'

Baggs's mouth hung open, his eyes were round as marbles. He looked at Doctor Flyte as if he was a total stranger. 'So you came back this time, just to get him?' said Baggs. 'To pay the doctor back? That's the only reason we got the boy and came here?'

'Yes. I thought the Mearbeck boy would settle him good and proper with his witchcraft – and you know why that was such a good joke?' Flyte glared at them. 'Because Sarah Mearbeck was Brittlebank's cousin!'

Reuben jumped as if a needle had jabbed him: *cousin*?

'Aye. Surprised? There's a laugh, using his cousin's magic to kill him – or it would have been, if it worked . . . And this'll surprise you even more, Skinny, I were at her hanging. Saw her. Saw you. I went by design. I was pleased to see her go, you understand? Came to cheer. A Mearbeck dead. What a lark! What a happy day – because I hate them all.'

Mearbeck, cousin to Brittlebank! His grandmother had told him to find his cousin in Stonebridge and he had, and never knew it! He tugged at the rope around his wrists. Too late! It was all happening too late!

Baggs scratched his head.

'No . . . I don't understand what it means.'

'I don't care what it means,' said Flyte, 'other than any Mearbeck or Brittlebank is a rat – pestilent, rotten, a devilish worm and deserves to be dead!' Flyte leaned back and shut his eyes, breathing heavily.

'It's a muddle,' said Baggs, slowly. 'You never said before. I don't know what to think.'

'You? You don't need think anything,' Flyte muttered. 'Why need I tell you? What use would the story have been to you? You with a brain no bigger than a chestnut? It's my business, only mine. Now, shut your pie-hole. It's not important for you to understand a jot.'

Flyte rolled over and almost immediately fell into a drunken sleep. Baggs built up the fire, wrapped himself in blankets and settled down close by.

Reuben tried again.

'Baggs?'

'What?'

'Just untie me, Baggs. He'd never know, you could say I got free on my own. You could do it. You don't want to be a murderer. Whatever else you've done, Baggs, you've never murdered anyone, have you?'

'Don't speak, boy,' Baggs said. 'You're no bigger'n a rasher of wind, but you muddle me. He muddles me. Here, take this.' He threw Reuben's cloak over him.

'Now be quiet. Don't try and talk or I might have to hurt you and shut you up proper.'

Silence descended.

When he heard them both snoring, Reuben began to feverishly tug and pull at the ropes that bound him to the wagon. He twisted and pulled but he was held too tightly and all that he managed to do was rub his skin raw.

He gazed into the fire, piecing together all that Flyte had told him.

As long as Flyte is not truly my father, I'll fight! Please God, please, don't let him be my father!

24
The Toadstone

Birdsong woke Reuben.

His cloak was damp, he was cold, his legs were twisted where the rope held him. He squinted up at the mistle thrush above him and automatically wished it 'good morning', for luck. The forest around him steamed. It glowed and glistened as if it had been freshly polished with beeswax.

The others were still asleep.

A tiny movement beside him caught his eye: hundreds of ants busy in the dead tree trunk. He watched them for a while as they hurried across the soft brown fungus, which sprouted like rabbits' ears on the rotting wood. They struggled over the lichen and battled through a tiny-leafed moss. It made him smile. A miniature world, perfectly ordered and all going on without me, he thought. It doesn't matter to them whether I live or die. It doesn't matter to anyone, anywhere. Everything will just go on the same, when I've left it . . .

He sat up.

No.

His arms ached. His legs ached. His head throbbed and he was hungry. But not ready to disappear.

I shan't let them do it! They've no right. My life's hardly begun. I shall fight! Lord, I'm cleverer than them! Younger. There must be something I can do. I will not be snuffed out like a worthless reed candle!

Ideas. Ideas. Granny, I need an idea!

He watched Baggs and Flyte slowly drifting into consciousness. Baggs fingered his bandage and stroked his cheek. Flyte had begun groaning, tossing and moaning – suddenly he shot upright and dashed into the bushes, one hand holding his stomach, the other pressed against his backside.

That brought Baggs fully awake.

'Poor doctor. Doctor Flyte ain't well,' he said to Reuben.

He started blowing on the embers and laying on fresh kindling. The flames soon danced and the wood crackled.

'How can he be ailing? Is his toadstone not working?' asked Reuben.

Baggs looked at him darkly. 'You're saucy, ain't you? The stone does work,' he said. 'He'd be worse if he didn't have it at all, eh? I suspect the air was bad in Stonebridge, or it were that mead, that swish water . . . 'Less you've done something to him.' He chewed on some black bread and stared at Reuben, thoughtfully.

Reuben stared back. I'm cleverer, he told himself. I've got the truth on my side. And Granny. I won't give up without a fight. An idea. Give me an idea!

Flyte came back. His shirt neck hung open, revealing his scrawny white chest and the leather pouch holding his amulet.

The toadstone! That was it! That was his weak spot. He only had to get that and Flyte would weaken. An idea! A spark of hope fizzed through him like a tinder flaring.

'What's the matter with you?' asked Baggs. 'You've got nothing to smile about. Shall I give him some bread, Doctor Flyte?'

'Don't need bread at the bottom of Cal's Cauldron.'

'We could leave him here,' said Baggs, setting out some potato cakes on a hot stone in the fire. 'We could tie him to a tree or something?'

'No, he'll blab.'

'I don't like the idea . . . I mean, throwing him in a hole and everything, that's real murder . . .'

'Yes, it's murder, so what?'

'Nothing, Doctor, nothing . . .'

'Thanks anyway, Baggs,' said Reuben.

'I don't want your thanks,' Baggs growled.

'Come on, then,' said Flyte. 'Let's move.'

Baggs untied the ropes that held Reuben to the wagon, but kept his hands tied. 'Come on.'

The track meandered along beside a river, then moved upwards over rougher ground where the rocks broke through the earth in pale heaps like broken teeth. They passed a tiny cottage with no roof or windows: long ago deserted, crumbling now and slowly being reclaimed by the forest.

'Old mining man used to live there,' said Flyte, nodding at the hut.

'I know,' said Baggs, then faltered, scratched his head and made a face. 'I mean, no, how could I know that?'

'Yes, how could you?' said Flyte. 'My old cat of an aunt told me the man would take me away if I misbehaved and drop me down the mine. Once, she let him dangle me right over the edge on a rope. Punishment, for stealing a bit of pie from the hearth. Only a morsel of pie! The old man near dropped me. Scratched deep onto my heart, that deed is.'

Reuben felt Baggs yank suddenly at the rope.

'Is that right?' Baggs asked. He sounded puzzled.

'It is,' said Flyte, coldly, 'She had no heart that woman, no heart at all.'

'Didn't she?' Baggs considered. There was confusion in his voice and Reuben wondered what it was that was bothering him so.

Something was bothering Reuben too; he was bursting with a peculiar energy, his heart was thumping and his chest was tight and full. Maybe it was lack of food that was making him so wild. He felt light enough to fly.

'So we're related, Flyte,' he said, hardly knowing what

he was going to say until the words popped out. 'And you're going to kill your own son?'

Flyte spun round and swiped Reuben round the head. 'Quiet! Stop that talk!'

But Reuben couldn't be quiet. Without warning, he burst into song:

'There were three ravens sat on a tree,
Down a down, hey down, hey down,
They were as black as black might be,
With a downnnnn,
The one of them said to his mate,
"Where shall we our breakfast take?"
With a down, derry, derry, derry down, down.'

Baggs jabbed him in the back with a stick, making Reuben stumble.

'Hush! Don't!'

But Reuben would not be stopped. He began the second verse even louder and stronger, stamping his feet as he sung.

'Down in yonder green field,
Down a down, hey down, hey down.
There lies a knight slain under his shield,
With a downnnnn,
His hounds they lie down at his feet,
So well they do their master keep.
With a down, derry, derry, derry down, down.'

Reuben sang the old song with much expression, the

way his grandmother used to. His 'downs' were low and long and sad. And when the song demanded it, his voice soared up into the sky.

Reuben stopped singing abruptly when they came to Cal's Cauldron. It was such a miserable place, such a deathly silent place that his mouth went dry and his head was suddenly drained of words.

Cal's Cauldron was a deep hole at the base of a sharp, stony crag over which trees and bushes grew. In places the tree roots were exposed, twisting and gnarled as they clawed their way back into the earth.

The hole was about six feet in diameter; a black, damp, forbidding place, too dark and deep to see into. It was ringed with holly bushes and briars and slabs of pale-yellow stone that reached down into its insides.

Flyte pushed through the leaves and stood close to the rim, peering down into its depths.

'On a rope,' he murmured, 'dangling over the edge. I were only six . . .' He threw a rock in. They heard it bump against the sides, then, while they held their breath, they heard it hit the bottom with a deep, faraway thud. 'What type of man could do that?'

Flyte looked round slyly at Reuben and smiled.

'No getting out of that one,' he said. 'Too steep to climb. It'll look like an accident if anyone were to find you, ever.'

Reuben's high spirits had drained away. Now he felt

weak and sick. There was no escape. He had to get Flyte's toadstone, but how?

Baggs had been strangely quiet, preoccupied and thoughtful since they passed the derelict cottage. Now he was staring round at the crag and Cal's Cauldron as if he hated the place. Reuben saw him watching Flyte from beneath the cover of his bandages; sidelong, suspicious. What was wrong with Baggs? What had changed?

'Are you feeling ill, Baggs?' Reuben asked him.

'Hush up! Doctor, it won't look like an accident with his hands tied,' said Baggs. 'If he's found, it'll look bad for us.'

'That's a point,' agreed Flyte. 'Come here, Stick.'

He took the rope from Baggs and though Reuben dug his heels hard into the earth, Flyte dragged and pulled him to the mouth of the pit. Cold, damp air oozed up from the hole, bringing an earthy smell of decay. Reuben began to shiver and whimper. He tried to stop, he hugged himself to keep still and get warm, to try and think, but he couldn't stop trembling. He'd never felt so sick and scared and wretched in his life.

He stared at the hole, imagining a pile of bodies down there, one on top of the other, nearly reaching right up to the very top . . .

Reuben tried to concentrate on just breathing. He had to keep breathing. He let his shoulders relax, tried to smile. This was his last chance. Lord, how his heart hurt and his throat ached. He had to do something. He faced Flyte, aware that his smile was slipping off his face, that his eyes were smarting with tears. He had to. Now!

'No! You shan't!' he cried.

He'd taken them by surprise.

He jumped to one side, tugging at the rope so suddenly that a length of it – a couple of feet long – slipped from Flyte's hands.

'Flyte! I'm cursed!' he cried. '*There were three ravens sat on a tree* . . . I can't die. They sold my soul to the Devil when I was a baby, I must live for ever. Baggs! Don't let him. I can do dark magic, Flyte, don't you want to see it? The most terrible retributions if you hurt me! Baggs! Baggs! I'll haunt you for the rest of your life! You mustn't! Don't!'

Flyte began to haul in the rope, but Baggs had already got hold of it.

'Untie him Baggs,' said Flyte, coldly, throwing the end of the rope to him. 'Get on with it. I'm tired of his voice!'

'You're not going to do it!' screamed Reuben. 'You know I can curse you. Think of your face, Baggs! Remember!'

Baggs was standing behind Reuben. Slowly, thoughtfully, he undid the knots at Reuben's wrists. His fingers fumbled, he hesitated, looking up at Flyte.

'Are you sure this is right, Doctor Flyte?' Baggs paused, 'I mean–'

The moment Reuben felt Baggs's concentration waver, he thrust his hands against the loosened knots and pushed the rope off.

He was free.

Quick as a flash, he flew at Flyte, scraping his nails into his face, pounding his fists into his stomach, rubbing his hard little head up against his chin.

Flyte was caught off guard. He fought, but Reuben was faster and more desperate. As Flyte sidestepped, avoiding the yawning hole, Reuben caught the leather pouch at his neck, wrapped his fingers round it and pulled. The thin strap broke.

'Got it!' He raised it in the air, swinging it wildly, dancing with glee. '*There were three ravens sat on a tree, Down a down, hey down, hey down!*'

Flyte froze. Every ounce of colour drained from his face, his jaw sagged. 'You devil!' he shrieked. 'Baggs! He took my stone!'

'Yes, call me devil!' cried Reuben, madly, glancing at Cal's Cauldron. 'Call me what you will. I don't care!' Reuben waved the pouch above his head. 'Watch!'

'*No!*' roared Flyte.

Laughing, Reuben hurled the leather bag into the chasm.

'There! Now you've no protection! Now my magic can work on you. Just as I put the curse on Baggs, now I shall do so to you! *Down, derry, derry, derry down, down!*'

Flyte slowly picked some leaves off his trousers. He stared calmly away, past Reuben, past Baggs. He was up to his trickery again, Reuben knew.

But Reuben was too wild and wonderful. 'A snail with no shell, that's you! Nothing to keep you safe! My powers are strong. Beware, Flyte, none of your quackery can save you now–'

Without warning, Flyte leaped at him, teeth bared, hands like claws.

They were dangerously close to the hole. Baggs leaped at Flyte, but only caught the corner of his jacket in his hand. There was a ripping sound as stitches broke. Baggs tumbled, fell forwards, knocking Flyte's feet from under him.

'You fool!' Flyte cried, falling.

Cal's Cauldron gaped beside him.

Wide-eyed, Flyte twisted and jerked, trying to avoid the hole, but his feet tangled in the brambles, they slipped on the rotten leaves and he slithered into the void, snatching at everything, anything; arms waving, hands flapping; he managed to just grasp and hold a knot of bracken. He hung, kicking and cursing, on the very edge of the hole.

'Help me, Baggs!' His face was all twisted and ugly. He slapped his hand onto the earth, tearing at the fronds of grass, uprooting stems and showering dirt. There was mud on his face, in his mouth. 'Help me!'

Baggs didn't move. He stared at Flyte, with a strange expression on his face: was he puzzled, horrified, alarmed? Reuben couldn't tell.

'Help me! My *son*!'

The words were like the lash of a whip and Reuben flinched, but still he didn't move.

Flyte's long fingers scrabbled at the grass, scratched desperately at the smooth rock, again and again, trying to fasten and grab hold. His lips were pulled back over his teeth in a terrible grimace, an expression that Reuben knew would be imprinted on his mind for ever and ever.

'Baggs! My son! Reuben! Reuben! For your grandmother's sake!'

Grandmother. Something snapped inside him and Reuben sprang forward, reaching out for Flyte. She wouldn't want this. 'Help me, Baggs!' Reuben said. 'Help me!'

But Baggs didn't move.

Reuben flung himself flat on the grass and grasped Flyte's sleeve. They were eyeball to eyeball, staring into each other's core. Reuben knew he had to catch hold of Flyte's hand, but – would Flyte pull him in? Would he?

Still they stared at each other.

A ripping sound, and Flyte's sleeve came away in Reuben's hand.

Flyte's fingers slipped through the wet grass, gliding

away, like an adder. He slithered smoothly, slowly, drifted almost, into the abyss.

His scream was muffled, desperate, dreadful. It seemed to last for hours, lingering, ringing in the stone, then there was a thud.

Silence.

Heart hammering, the scream ricocheting round his head, Reuben dragged himself away from the pit.

Baggs was lying on the ground. He met his blank, round-eyed gaze. Baggs hadn't helped. Why hadn't he helped?

'It was an accident,' said Baggs.

'An accident,' Reuben repeated.

'He slipped.'

It was suddenly too much. Reuben crumpled. Flyte was dead. He hadn't helped. He'd called for his son to help him and no one had come. No one should die like that.

'I'm sorry!' Reuben shouted. 'Forgive me!'

The two of them sat, without moving or speaking. Occasionally their eyes would meet, then they'd quickly look away.

They were finished.

25
Doctor Brittlebank and the Jewel in the Toad

Much later, a dog's shrill barking and men's voices calling woke them from their stupor.

Reuben recognised the barks: Shadow!

The scruffy dog burst through the trees and flung herself at Reuben, wagging her tail, yelping and whining with excitement.

'Good girl!' Reuben cried, hugging her tightly. Shadow rubbed her wet nose into his neck and licked his face. 'So smelly,' Reuben murmured. 'Such a fine, smelly dog. Where did you go? Where've you been?'

The voices were getting nearer, but he couldn't move – his legs were like jelly, his mouth dry . . . It was over for him. The running away and the hiding. 'I'll just stay here with you, Shadow,' he whispered. 'We'll be together, hey? You and me?'

So the three of them stayed there at that terrible place until four men appeared – one was Doctor Brittlebank.

'Well, look at that!' cried Brittlebank. 'We've found them. That's what the dog was after – you two lads!' He stared at Reuben and then at Baggs, taking in their white, tear-stained faces and dull silence. 'Where's that scoundrel Flyte?'

Reuben shook his head and pointed into Cal's Cauldron. 'He fell,' he said.

'My God!' cried the doctor. 'The poor soul!'

The men shuffled close to the mouth of Cal's Cauldron and peered down, warily.

'Not the first, probably,' said one.

'Many tales of people disappearing here,' said another, gruffly. 'Unwanted babies and such. Not a nice place.'

Reuben shuddered.

'Nobody would survive that fall,' said Brittlebank. 'Not even the Devil himself. Ah, well, I'm cheated out of seeing him go to court and be properly punished, but there . . .' He stared at Baggs. 'What's the matter with him?'

'Shock, I think,' said Reuben.

'And you, boy, I suppose you thought I might be dead,' he asked.

Reuben flushed. 'Yes. No, I mean, I hoped not. I didn't mean to,' he said. 'It was Flyte meant you to be dead.'

'Well, as you can see, I am not. We'll talk about that later. Who is this person? He wasn't at the fair,' said the Doctor, pointing at Baggs.

Baggs shook his head and wouldn't speak.

'He was hiding, because of the bandage,' Reuben explained. 'His name is Baggs.'

Doctor Brittlebank stared hard at Baggs, looking him up and down. 'Very well, he can talk later. Come with us, both of you, you've questions to answer.'

They made their way back slowly to the doctor's house.

Reuben found himself walking right behind Doctor Brittlebank. He studied the back of the doctor's head, the shape of his ears, the way he walked, wondering if there was anything similar in his own body and movement. He wished he dared to ask him if he had a birthmark at the base of his neck.

I'll never dare tell him we're related, thought Reuben. If we really are. If it wasn't another of Flyte's lies. Oh, but I hope it is true. I hope I can be forgiven and stay in Stonebridge and I won't have to move on.

They passed the broken wagon. Nellie whinnied at them.

'We must look after her,' said Reuben, anxiously. 'She'll be hungry and thirsty. She's a good horse. Can we take her back?'

'Of course, we must,' said the doctor. 'I suppose she's Flyte's property so what will become of her, I don't know, but we can't leave her here.'

The larger of the men took Nellie by the halter and led her back along the lane with them.

'She can be stabled with my horse until we've got everything sorted out,' said Doctor Brittlebank.

The doctor's house was on the edge of Stonebridge. It

was the nicest house that Reuben had ever been in and by far the grandest. There were wooden planks on the floor so it was warm and smooth and springy to walk on, there was furniture covered in rich fabric. Even tapestries hanging on the wall. A room full of books. How his granny would have loved that.

Reuben wasn't afraid. He wasn't angry, sad, worried. He was nothing. Every emotion seemed to have been knocked out of him. He sat on a wooden bench beside the fire and stroked Shadow who had come to sit with him. He occupied himself pulling burrs and twigs from the dog's coat and chucking them in the fire. He was sure he would be punished and there wasn't anything he could do to prevent it. Anything would be better than being tipped down a dark hole and being left to rot in the ground.

Shadow laid her long head across Reuben's knee, looking up at him with her knowing, trusting brown eyes, her tail gently polishing the floor.

'That's a fine dog,' Doctor Brittlebank said. 'How did you come by her? Did Flyte steal her?'

Reuben looked up at him in surprise. 'Oh, no, sir. Flyte didn't like dogs. The dog found us,' he said, 'when we were in Longford. She followed us all the time on our way here. That's why I call her Shadow.'

'She's in a pitiful state,' said the doctor, rumpling the dog's ears. 'Didn't you feed her or brush her?'

'Well . . .' Reuben began, then looked down at his own clothes, torn, dirty and ragged. His filthy hands.

'Yes, I do see,' said Doctor Brittlebank, a small smile crossing his face. 'You are also in a pitiful state.'

'I fed her when I could and anyway, she wasn't always with us. I don't know how she managed, really I don't. She was a shadow.'

'I see . . . Where do you come from, boy?'

'Birtwell Priory,' said Reuben, forgetting to lie. Then he remembered and his heart sank lower. That was so stupid! Now the doctor would find out about his grandmother being hanged. But he wanted to tell him about his grandmother. He felt this man would understand – and if Sarah Mearbeck truly had been his cousin, he had to tell him so. Maybe he'd be sent back to his village. No, not to witness those Silvers in his cottage, using his front door and trampling over his garden. He'd never go back and live beside Meg Silver. Never. Why hadn't he lied?

'I had a relative in Birtwell Priory,' said the doctor.

Reuben glanced at him. Dare he tell him? He wanted to desperately, but the doctor went on. 'Are you hungry?'

'Very, sir.'

'Well, help yourself,' he told him, as a maid brought in some ale and cold meats and bread. 'And you, Baggs. Come nearer to the fire. Aren't you cold?'

But Baggs didn't respond. His eyes were dull and

distant, as if he was listening to something far away that no one else could hear.

'Thank you,' said Reuben, tearing off some soft white bread. It melted in his mouth, it was like eating a cloud. 'I am a little hungry.'

'That dog doesn't take her eyes off you. Strange how she follows your every move,' Doctor Brittlebank said. 'Here, have some ale to wet your whistle. Now, where d'you say you first saw her?'

Reuben told him about the appearance of the dog in Longford and the way she had followed him. 'I liked to imagine she was there whenever I was sad,' Reuben told him. 'Like a guardian angel, she was, if a dog can be an angel.'

'I don't see why not . . .'

'At the fair,' Reuben interrupted, 'you were just pretending to collapse, weren't you? For a moment, I thought I'd really made the potion poisonous!'

Doctor Brittlebank chuckled. 'Yes. It suddenly seemed such a good opportunity to show up that charlatan for what he was – you did a good bit of pretending with your toad eating too!'

'I had to,' said Reuben. 'In truth, I did. He'd have killed me if I hadn't, wouldn't he, Baggs?'

Baggs slumped further into his seat and pushed his chin into his chest. He didn't respond.

'The likes of Flyte should be locked up,' said Doctor

Brittlebank. 'He wasn't an ignorant man, but misguided and bad. He encouraged people's suspicious and dreads. He took money from them on false pretences. I'm a real doctor, Reuben. I try as hard as I can to be a good doctor too. I despise quacks.'

There! Another chance for him to tell the doctor that his grandmother was his cousin. Reuben almost spoke out, but couldn't. But who am I? he thought. Maybe the son of a rogue so how can I expect Doctor Brittlebank to accept me?

'I remember Flyte when he was a boy here,' the doctor told them. 'His aunt was not a good woman. She didn't want him. Nobody wanted Bartholomew Flyte. Can you imagine what that's like, not to be wanted? For nobody to care whether you live or die? He never had any luck. He married – had to, if you get my meaning – but his young wife ran away, leaving a baby boy . . .'

'No!' Reuben cried without meaning to. Baby Reuben! It had to be him. It was the worst thing that Doctor Brittlebank could have said.

'Flyte had the child looked after at Mother Margaret's. She looked after all the unwanted, orphaned babes.'

Baggs suddenly burst out with a loud sob and buried his head in his hands, as if Flyte's story was too sad to bear.

'Are you well?' asked Reuben. 'Does the wound hurt? He got a fish hook in his cheek, sir. And Flyte's dead . . .

They were partners, well, in a manner, except that Flyte told him what to do . . .'

'So you're from Birtwell Priory? That was where my cousin Sarah lived. I don't know when you left the place, but she was hanged recently on some ridiculous, trumped up charge of witchcraft!' Doctor Brittlebank stood up and paced around the room. 'I heard about Sarah Mearbeck's trial, but news travels so slowly. I set off to try and do something, but by the time I reached Willsbridge it was too late, she was dead. They didn't even give her a proper trial. I would have done anything to help her!'

Reuben's heart throbbed and pulsed expectantly. This was the moment to speak, but what could he say? The doctor had as good as proved that Reuben was Flyte's son.

'I thought this country was getting more tolerant – looking more into the future,' said Doctor Brittlebank. 'It distressed me enormously to hear of her death. She was a good woman. Even when she lived here, she was famous for making wonderful healing potions and for her midwifery skills.'

'Yes, I know,' said Reuben.

The doctor didn't hear him. 'The strange thing is, her grandson was put into Mother Margaret's cottage too, come to think of it, when her daughter and son-in-law both died of the fever. I remember her coming back to collect it. A boy, it was. That would be about ten years ago, now . . .'

'Doctor Brittlebank, that was me,' said Reuben. 'I hope you don't think that I'm making it up, or trying to say I'm your family, when you don't want more family, or anything like that, but–'

'You? Sarah's grandson? Explain yourself, young man.'

'Sarah Mearbeck was my grandmother,' Reuben said, and then went on to tell him about her trial and her death. 'Flyte lied. He said I was his son! I knew I wasn't! It was a trick to try and keep me. And she told me, before she died, that I should come to Stonebridge and find you, and now I have.'

'Flyte's dead!' said Baggs, suddenly.

'Are you all right, young Baggs?' asked Doctor Brittlebank. 'Is there anything we can do to help you? I'll make him a drink of valerian to soothe him. The shock's been too much. See how pale he is. And I should look under that rag around your head and see if I can help you. What happened?'

Baggs shook his head. 'No, no,' he muttered, squeezing his eyes shut, as if trying to see some picture hidden in his head. 'This is all mixed up. I remember being on the end of a rope,' he said, quietly, 'hanging down into the blackness. I remember it now. *Are you scared? Are you wetting yourself, little caw-baby?*' Tears escaped from his eyes and rolled down his face. '*Oh, I bet you're scared!*

Shall I drop you? Will the rope snap? Stop that snivelling, little dollop or I'll let go the rope!'

'Baggs, what are you talking about?' said Reuben, staring at him anxiously. 'You're confused. That's Flyte's story. It wasn't you!'

Baggs sighed. He wiped at his tears. 'It's no matter,' he said eventually. 'I'm talking nonsense, ain't I? It were Doctor Flyte dangled down the hole, ain't that so? You needn't worry about me. It wasn't me. I'm just dreaming, I must be. I've got mixed up. I don't think straight.' He got up and lurched towards the door. 'I'm going.'

'No! Don't!' cried Doctor Brittlebank. 'Where will you go, Baggs? What will you do? You need help. Let me see to your face.'

'I don't need you!' he spat back, but he didn't move.

'Wait, do wait,' said the doctor. 'I want to help you.'

Baggs sighed and sat down again and when Doctor Brittlebank brought water and clean rags and slowly began to take the bandages off Bagg's face, he didn't complain.

'Your spots are much better, Baggs,' said Reuben. 'And the cut's not too bad considering everything, though it's sort of pulled your face sideways a bit – where the edges have joined it's a bit funny, crooked.' The last of the rags came away. 'I wish I could have stitched it– Oh!'

'What is it?' asked Doctor Brittlebank.

'Flyte!' cried Reuben, staring at Baggs. 'Your face is twisted – Oh, oh, Baggs!'

Baggs put his hand up to his face and felt the scar tissue gingerly. It was mending, but as Reuben said, in healing the flesh of the cheek had pulled tight, making his face lopsided . . . making his resemblance to Flyte show through. 'Now I see it. It was you! He was your father! Flyte said you hadn't got a father, but he lied. It was him!'

'I knew,' said Baggs, dully. 'When we were at Cal's Cauldron, I remembered all sorts of things. It was me he put down there. It was me he hated and despised and . . . I remember him coming to get me. From that place with the cradle that the baby was tossed out of? I was young – five or so. I do remember and he thought I didn't. And I did remember you, Reuben, 'cos of your mark. Old Mother Margaret said it was a wild strawberry stuck inside you, bursting out. And I remember your granny.'

'How?'

'She came and got you and she mended us. I mean, she did these special things, like to a little girl what was there, she put these soggy leaves all piled up on her arm where she had a boil and the boil mended. She gave us a special green herb drink to make us strong. We thought she was a sort of . . . fairy or queen or something. That's why I remember the mark, 'cos she asked specially for the baby with the mark and we all pointed you out.

Fancy. Ain't that weird?' He shook his head sadly. ' 'Course, I knew Flyte weren't your father.'

Doctor Brittlebank brought Baggs a drink of brandy instead of the valerain he'd mentioned and Baggs sipped it thoughtfully. 'I did have a father,' he whispered, 'it was all I ever wanted, a father, and he kept it from me.'

'What about that birthmark on his neck that was like mine?' asked Reuben.

'A poultice dyed red from berries. He thought it were such a joke. We noticed that mark the first night in The Longford Arms, remember?'

Reuben nodded. 'But why?'

''Cos he wanted to curse and hex folk and he thought you had them powers. He were going to bind you to him, body and soul.'

Reuben and Baggs both slept at Doctor Brittlebank's house that night, on the softest mattresses covered with fine, clean linen.

Shadow lay across Reuben's feet – just like the hound in the song – keeping his master safe. When Reuben woke in the night, which he did many times, he could reach out and touch her rough fur. It was reassuring that she never moved from her place by him. He even didn't mind the smell; just smelling it meant she was close.

'Faithful one,' he whispered. 'Now we're together. You never need leave. My Shadow dog, we've come home.'

Nobody heard Baggs go, but some time in the night he disappeared, taking Nellie with him. Shadow must have heard him, but she didn't bark, as if she knew that Baggs wanted to slip away like that, and Reuben might have stopped him.

'I'm glad he's gone,' said the doctor. 'I didn't know what I was going to do with him. He was an unhappy soul. He's got the horse. Probably he'll take that old wagon if he can fix it. And if he's any sense he'll get it back on the road – he's got transport and maybe a livelihood selling potions!'

'And I will never buy one!' said Reuben, grimly.

In the days that followed, Reuben thought about Baggs and their dreadful time beside Cal's Cauldron, often.

He tried to remember each moment.

Had Baggs been trying to save Flyte early on, when his jacket tore? Or by then had he realised that Flyte was his father and understood how badly he'd been treated, and pushed him? And why didn't Baggs try and save him at the end, when he was almost certain of his relationship to Flyte.

My son! he'd called. And his son was there and it was too late.

One day in the summer, Reuben found a dead toad beside the path and took it to show the doctor. 'This creature, this Bufo bufo–'

'Latin, that's all,' said Brittlebank, smiling.

'This toad has been the cause of many of my problems,' went on Reuben. 'I would like to study it. To look inside it and find its jewel.'

'I have dissected many toads and frogs, Reuben, and you do not see a toadstone around my neck.'

'Perhaps only certain toads hold a magic stone?'

Doctor Brittlebank led Reuben into his study. This was where he made up remedies, kept his bandages and books, his new microscope and tiny metal surgical tools. It was a wonderful room, one that Reuben wanted desperately to explore and understand.

The doctor took the dead amphibian and laid it out on a dissecting board, stretching and pinning its limbs into the soft wax covering the wooden board. Very carefully and precisely, he dissected it while Reuben watched every move. One day I'll do clever things like that, he vowed.

At last Doctor Brittlebank came to the head of the toad. He snipped back the skin, showed Reuben the network of veins and bones, the optic nerves, eyes and brain stem. He opened up the tiny skull and taking a magnifying glass, urged Reuben to look for its magical toadstone.

'You may keep what you find, Reuben.'

Reuben searched and searched. 'There's nothing there!' he said at last. 'But everyone knows . . .'

'Ah, yes, everyone knows.' Doctor Brittlebank smiled. 'Everyone knows, but do they bother to find out? It's just a myth, like iron in the bed will ward off witches, like swallows spend the winter sleeping in the mud, like spilt salt will summon the Devil,' said Doctor Brittlebank. 'All stories. There's nothing magical about toads, except perhaps their eyes.'

'Their eyes?'

'Why, yes, they can shine like jewels, Reuben, have you never noticed? They have such remarkable eyes, people imagine they reflect something magical inside.'

'And yet there was nothing there,' said Reuben.

'Well, isn't that the same with so many things,' said the doctor, calmly. 'We look and see so much more than there really is, because we want more. We want secrets and powerful stones and magical jewels. Of course, on other occasions, we look and see nothing and yet there is so much that we miss.'

'Doctor Flyte trusted his life to that toadstone,' said Reuben. 'Pepperday sold it to him. He was such a nice fellow too. Will people ever stop being superstitious?'

'One day, perhaps,' said the doctor, with a smile.

Reuben found that Doctor Brittlebank could explain most things but he couldn't explain Shadow. There was no scientific or medical explanation for her behaviour.

On the day that Doctor Brittlebank was to formerly adopt Reuben as his son and heir – the day he promised to help Reuben become a doctor – Shadow behaved as normal. She followed Reuben, her head within easy reach of his hands for stroking, as she always did, nudging against his side. She watched him, as she always did, slinking along behind him whenever he went out of the room. Her eyes followed his every move: she sat when he sat, lay down when he lay down. She wagged her tail whenever he spoke to her or whenever she heard his voice, as she always did. But when evening came and she scratched at the door, Reuben let her out with a heavy heart, which he couldn't account for.

He didn't want her to go.

'Good girl,' he whispered. 'Don't be long.' And Shadow had turned, lifted her head and something, something, which Reuben thought was a smile, had flickered across her sweet face, reminding him, how strange, how odd – of his grandmother.

And she never came back.